Praise for the Melanie Hogan Mystery Series

Shear Madness

"Great story – Took a twist at the end that I hadn't anticipated! Rhonda writes in a way that helps the reader visualize the scene – makes it a very fun read and even more suspenseful. I'm ready for the next one in the series!"

Shear Madness

"It was an excellent read, caught your attention at the beginning and held it to the end. Likable characters that are well developed. Rhonda Blackhurst has a way of writing that is very visual."

Shear Madness

"Loved this cozy mystery and can't wait for the next one in the series. Melanie is a charming character, the dialogue is witty and funny, and the mystery has a twist I didn't guess."

Shear Deception

"Wonderfully written, kept me in suspense!"

Shear Deception

"Once again Rhonda has written an excellent mystery. Her characters come alive, you feel you know them personally. She gets you interested from the first page and keeps you to the last page. A very good read."

Shear Deception

"Melanie Hogan's story continues in this next book in the series - and Blackhurst does not disappoint. All the lovable characters are back, and one that's not so lovable-a surprising foe to Melanie's sweet character."

Shear Murder

"Very enjoyable cozy mystery. The dialogue draws the reader into the story and helps to develop the characters and story development. I was drawn in from the beginning. The main character attended a reunion gathering of old friends when the unthinkable happens. Great who-done-it with likable characters and a surprising ending. Highly recommended."

Shear Holiday Mayhem

A Melanie Hogan Mystery
Book 5

Rhonda Blackhurst

Books may be purchased in quantity and/or special sales by contacting the author at www.rhondablackhurst.com or rjblackhurst0611@gmail.com.

Published by Lighthouse Press, Colorado
Cover Design by: No Sweat Graphics & Formatting

Library of Congress Control Number: 2020920297
ISBN-13: 978-1-7359393-0-8
ISBN-10: 1-7359393-0-7

First Edition
Printed in the United States of America

Also by Rhonda Blackhurst

To Ben and Alex. You are the son-shine to my soul. Always. No matter what.

And she gave birth to her firstborn son; and she wrapped Him in cloths, and laid Him in a manger, because there was no room for them in the inn.

Luke 2:7

1

Good Lord, what have I done?

I groaned when I turned the corner into the plaza parking lot that housed my hair salon, A Cut Above. This afternoon was the plaza's sixth annual Christmas Festival and the first one we'd decided to contribute by giving free services rather than discounted product. When I had left to run an errand a mere hour ago during a scheduled break in the action, everything was status quo. Now a line of customers snaked around the building's side and then back out into the parking lot. The line appeared to sway as the people shivered and huddled together. There was still an hour to go before the activities even began!

Claire, my best friend and co-owner of the salon, pulled up next to me in her bright orange Honda CRV. I could see that thing coming a mile away, and it fit her bubbly personality to a T. She'd run home to check on her nine-year-old daughter, Syd, who was with the sitter. The rest of the ladies should be arriving back any time now. We had all penciled a break into our schedules before the nightmare before Christmas began at one.

Claire pulled up so her driver's side was parallel to mine. We rolled our windows down. She noticed the look of panic on my face because she laughed.

"How is this *new* Melanie working out for you?" she asked, quickly glancing at the line then back at me. "Because remember the one who used to be satisfied with the mundane? I'm kind of missing her right about now."

My life used to be the epitome of routine. Heck, I had the stability gig down pat. That is until a couple of short years ago when I made a wish. Apparently, I made the wish as a star was falling because it came true. That wish? For my life to have a little excitement. Some spontaneity. I got that and more. Dead bodies started appearing, and I'd found myself a suspect a time or two.

"Claire, we can't let these people stand outside for another hour. They'll freeze to death." I studied the line and shook my head. "It's one of the coldest days we've had in weeks." And in northern Minnesota, that said something. Yikes!

"You and your brilliant ideas," she said, chuckling, her eyes glued to the line, now longer by two people.

"Why didn't you just say no when I suggested it?" I asked.

"For two reasons, my dear friend. First, you wouldn't have listened. Second, you wouldn't have listened." I made a face at her. "I'm giving you a hard time, but this is a good thing you're doing. It's sweet."

"I am not sweet," I scoffed. "And free haircuts and manicures from one to five will not accommodate all of these people. It'll take us until midnight."

"Which is why they're here an hour early. So they have a better chance of getting in. This isn't unlike Black Friday."

"Good thing we got a good night's sleep last night and scheduled breaks for ourselves before the madness begins, huh?" She didn't say anything, so I glanced at her. "You did get a good night's sleep, right? Because I can't have you dying on me in there. I'll prop you up beside your station and sing the song, 'Prop Me Up Beside the Jukebox if I Die.'"

Claire snorted. "Yeah, yeah. You've told me that a time or two. Your singing alone would wake me up. From the dead, even."

I made another face at her. "Come on, partner. Sitting here isn't getting anything done."

Our salon and a large grocery store chain bookended the mall, with several small businesses in between, two of them insurance agencies. Each company contributed something, however little, to

3

the event. For the most part, each one did their best to make it memorable and festive.

"Can you start early?" Someone shouted as we sliced through the line to get to the door.

"It's freezing out here!" Someone else complained. "Let us in."

I turned to face them. "We don't have enough room inside the salon for everyone." I turned to Claire and mumbled, "I sure didn't prepare for this."

"Never thought I'd see the day you weren't prepared," she mumbled back.

"Listen," I told the grumbling crowd, "Come to the front desk in the order you're standing in line. We'll sign you in, and then you can go to the grocery store or wait in your car until we begin."

"Aw, come on, lady," a man grumbled from the back of the line. "Can't you get started early? I'll never get in before five otherwise."

I glanced at Claire, who was giving me *the* look. "No," I mouthed. I know my friend well enough to know what she was thinking. She would have done free cuts and manicures for an entire week just to be sure we served everyone. Her heart was enormous, and it's gotten her into trouble a time or two.

"Come on, lady, what'd ya say?"

"First of all," I said, looking directly at the outspoken gentleman, "my name isn't lady, it's Melanie. Second of all, we have things we need to do before starting. But if you don't get in today, you're certainly welcome to make an appointment for another day."

"Yeah, but then I'll have to pay for it," he grumbled.

I gave him the most delightful smile I could muster, which wasn't great, then glanced at Claire.

"Breathe," she whispered.

Claire stationed herself behind the front counter, making sure everyone signed in. I marched back toward the office, admiring the white Christmas lights strung throughout the salon. Lights were my favorite part of Christmas. And the music, much to Babs and Rubie's dismay. They objected to starting Christmas music in the salon the day after Thanksgiving, but I did it anyway. One year I even started before Thanksgiving.

From the office, I could hear grumbling from the front of the salon. I hung my coat and scarf on the hook behind the door and went back to the reception counter to help Claire. Two women standing in line caught my attention. One was strikingly beautiful in a severe kind of way, probably more plastic on her than

5

a water bottle factory. The other was pretty small but appeared as if she could hold her own. What she couldn't hold was her mouth. She was giving the plastic barbie doll quite a tongue lashing. The string of people kept the door open, making us privy to their exchange as they stood only a few feet from the entrance.

Barbie turned toward the other woman and leaned forward, her face mere inches from her. "Listen here, you simpleton, I do not have to take this from you. I know people who know people."

"Is that a threat?" the woman said, her eyes narrow slits. "Because if it is, I'll — "

"Patti," Claire said with bright enthusiasm. Barbie startled and eyeballed Claire, apparently unaware she was standing in front of the counter. "You're next," Claire said. "Go ahead and sign your name and contact info." She handed her the pen.

"You already have my contact info," Patti said to Claire. "And you know I only let you touch my hair. I will get you, correct?"

It sounded like she was a teacher talking to a student. Claire gave me a subtle nudge.

"Yes," she said. "It might mean you have to wait a bit longer, but I will do my best to get you in on time."

Patti huffed and shook her head. "Okay, fine. As long as you do it."

Claire smiled, nodded her head, and handed the pen to the woman who'd been arguing with Patti. The woman elbowed Patti out of the way and snarled, "Come on, you biddy. Other people are waiting, you know."

I stayed long enough to see the woman sign her name. Trudy Flynn. I'd need to keep my eye on these two if they end up in the salon at the same time. For Patti being so set on Claire doing her hair, I couldn't remember seeing her in the salon before. Surely I would have remembered her. I nudged Claire with my shoulder and raised an eyebrow when she glanced at me.

She bent over close to my ear. "She's the one I come in early for because she doesn't like anyone to see her with chemicals. Wants everyone to think it's natural."

I almost snorted and shook my head. I wasn't sure there was much about her that was natural. "Want me to take over here?" I asked.

"No, no. Go ahead and get other stuff ready. I've got this covered."

I grabbed her coat, which she'd shed on the chair moments ago.

"It's freezing with that door standing open. Want to keep your coat?"

"Nah, I'm fine."

She had on a bright red turtleneck sweater over a green and red mini skirt with matching tights. I shrugged.

"Okay, then."

I strolled back to the office and hung her coat on the back of the door next to mine. I threw the towels from the washer into the dryer and tossed another load into the machine. Towels were a never-ending cycle, but it was a job none of us minded. Especially folding them fresh from the dryer in the wintertime as we clung to the heat.

"Hey there!"

I jumped at Rubie's voice behind me, hitting my head on the dryer door. "Ouch!" I yelped.

Rubie giggled. She was another stylist and one who'd fit in mine and Claire's circle quickly and perfectly. "You were stuck so far in the dryer I could have closed the door and shut you in."

"Not so," I said, rubbing my head, stopping when I looked at her. She was a ball of pink from head to toe. A bright pink fuzzy sweater hung just below her hips over a pair of pale pink skinny jeans with pink knee boots. Rubie loved pink, but this was excessive even for her. "You changed clothes?"

She grinned, revealing perfectly straight white teeth behind pink glossed lips. Her blond curls were pulled into a loose ponytail, tendrils flowing around her face. "Yeah. And I see you eyeing my boots. You know you want 'em." She kicked one up, inspected it briefly, then put it back down.

I wrinkled my nose. "Yeah, I don't think so."

She shook her head. "Stop looking at me like that, or I'll stuff you in the dryer."

I chuckled. "You look like a giant bottle of Pepto Bismol. And you won't stuff me in the dryer because you'd have to handle all that madness out there this afternoon without my help," I said, nodding toward the front door. I shook my head slowly. "I don't know what I was thinking. I certainly didn't expect what's out there."

"Connie's coming back, right?"

"She'd better. She just ran home to let her dog out. Babs will handle the manicures, so we'll be good. I think. I just hadn't expected the crowd to be so—"

"Grumpy?" she asked, jumping in to fold towels.

"Yeah. I mean, it's Christmas, for crying out loud."

Rubie shrugged. "It's only for four hours. We can do it."

I rolled my eyes. "Oh, to be young again."

Connie was the only one who has been with us since the very beginning when we opened the salon. Babs filled the vacant manicure job after an unfortunate series of events with other nail techs. And Rubie came to the salon about a year and a half ago, but it felt like she'd always been there.

"You're wearing those this afternoon?" Rubie asked me, pointing to my high heeled black boots. "Did you bring something else to change into?

"No. Why would I? I'm used to these."

She rolled her eyes. "You're going to be dying in them by five o'clock. And you'll be begging for my boots."

I laughed loudly. "Not a chance! And if I die in my boots, then I'll die happy. Be sure to bury me in them." I smiled obnoxiously at her.

She scrunched up her face. "You're such a nerd."

"Says the bottle of Pepto." I handed her an armful of towels. "Here's some more for you to fold. But don't hold them close to you. Not everyone wants to smell like Loves Baby Soft."

I hadn't even known they still made Loves Baby Soft perfume until Rubie started working at the salon. Sometimes I swear she bathes in the stuff.

"I don't know why I put up with you," she said.

"Because you love me." I gave her my best innocent look.

"You're hard not to love," she said, snickering. "Even when you're your usual sarcastic self."

"Especially then, huh?" I asked, winking at her.

By the time Connie and Babs strolled in, Claire was done signing people in and had locked the door again until one o'clock when we opened for the mad rush. She had given each a guesstimated time to come back, but most of them lingered outside the door instead of waiting in their cars. A few of them strolled on down the mall.

The businesses in the plaza were all finishing their festival set up. I peered through the window at the Christmas decorations: an enormous inflatable Christmas dragon, a Santa, two elves, an enormous lighted tree, and a live nativity scene. Thank goodness the baby Jesus wasn't live. I wrapped my arms around my waist and shivered, thinking of a baby out in the cold all afternoon. A man in a Santa hat was already ringing the bell for donations in front of the

11

grocery store. I always felt guilty if I walked by without giving something.

Further down was Santa's village, the chair still vacant. An elf fluttered around setting up the cookie and hot chocolate table. Yum! I knew where I would be visiting throughout the day. As hard as I try to limit sugar, the desire to eat it is greater, and my self-control goes out the window. Thank goodness my metabolism is good.

An old, faded, once-red Chevrolet El Camino pulled into the parking lot and rolled into a parking space. Moments later, Santa unfolded from the front seat, straightened his belt, then his beard, surveyed his surroundings, and headed toward his designated spot.

I jumped at a knock on the window. "Come on," the person yelled loud enough for me to hear through the glass. "Open up!"

I pointed to my watch, raised a finger, and mouthed, "One o'clock." Which, to my surprise, was only five more minutes.

I turned to look at the salon, making sure everything and everyone was ready. The twinkling Christmas lights and the decorated tree in the corner of the waiting area warmed me from the inside. As if on cue, all five of us met in the center of the salon. I put my hand out, palm down. The others layered their hands over mine in the middle of the circle.

"Let's roll, ladies," I said.

2

As soon as Claire opened the door, all heck broke loose. And it should have been our cue to cancel the event.

Despite Claire's suggestion to wait in cars or partake of the festivities down the mall after they checked in, the line formed again. People elbowed their way between each other, forcing their way toward the front. Amidst all the pushing and shoving—and more than an occasional curse word—my attention was drawn to Patti and Trudy Flynn, who had managed to stand next to each other in line again. *Both gluttons for punishment or what*? I wondered.

"This cannot be a coincidence," I mumbled.

"What?" Claire asked, looking toward the object of my attention. "Oh, good Lord," she said under her breath. "Trudy isn't up for a while yet. As in quite a while. Neither is Patti since they checked in one right after the other."

"You might want to tell *them* that," I said. "We probably should have given them a return time separate from one another."

Connie took the first client, Rubie the second, and Babs called for the first manicure client. I opened my mouth to say a name when a shriek pierced through the chatter.

"What the heck is—" I started.

Claire rushed past me. "Patti," she said as she pushed through the people blocking the doorway.

I followed close on her heels. Trudy reached for Patti's hair and yanked. I grimaced. *Ouch*! Patti's diet soda bottle flew from her hands. She reached to catch it and knocked a cup of hot cocoa from the hands of the woman behind her. Claire and I both froze as Patti's feet slipped out from beneath her. Patti landed on her behind, and the cocoa fell on her head and trailed down her face, taking the makeup with it.

"I'll get you for this, Trudy!" Patti screeched.

"People," I said, meeting resistance as I directed them away from the action scene. "Please go on down the mall until your turn is up."

"Aw, come on!" More than one complained. "That broad had it comin'!"

I stared at them in disbelief. "Excuse me?"

"She did!" Another insisted. "She's had it comin' for years."

I glanced at Claire, who, for a rare moment, was not smiling. A man I recognized as an employee at the bakery, Tim, handed Patti her diet soda bottle.

"Thank you, Tim," Claire said as she held onto Patti's elbow to help her stand.

"You," Patti hissed at Trudy when she was back on her feet. "You will pay for this. Why don't you ask your husband about—"

"Come on, Patti," Claire interrupted, stopping another scuffle. "Let's go inside and get you cleaned up."

"Ask my husband about what?" Trudy taunted. "I'm the one he chose, remember? Me! Not you." I stood by Trudy, my arm straight and tight in front of her, trying to be sure the separation between the two remained intact, which was becoming more and more difficult.

Claire and I shot each other a look, and Claire frowned. Patti twisted the cap on the soda bottle, and Claire slid her hand over it with lightning speed.

"Don't open that yet," Claire sputtered. "You'll have a bigger mess on your hands. And on me. The bottle's been shaken. Give it a few minutes to settle down."

"It's already been opened," Patti said, as she jerked her arm away from Claire. "You'll have to do my hair right away now." She held her arms out and peered down at herself then at Claire. "You can't expect me to stay like this for a moment longer." Patti glared at Trudy, who stifled a smirk. Miserably at that. "You know I'll get you back, you evil woman," Patti threatened. "When you're least expecting it."

"Come on," Claire said to Patti, leading her as gently as she could, her hand lightly on her back. Claire peered at me, rolled her eyes, shook her head slightly, and then focused on Patti again. "Let's get you a hot cup of fresh coffee, and you can use the restroom to clean up."

"I'm never going to get my haircut at this rate," someone hollered out.

"Come on! Time's a tickin'," another yelled.

"People," Rubie said from the doorway, "you're not getting in any faster by standing here screaming at us. In fact, you might not get in at all. So go, do your thing and come back at the time you were given."

I restrained myself from clapping and enveloping her in a bear hug. Instead, I gave her a discreet low-five and took a customer back to my chair.

After my first customer left and opened the door to go, I saw a police cruiser pull into the parking lot, and out came Cole, police officer with Birch Haven PD, and who had been assigned event security for this afternoon. Better late than never. He adjusted his duty belt as he stood.

Cole is Claire's boyfriend and was a lost cause from the moment they met. Sometimes watching him swoon over her made my stomach lurch. Claire would argue that my boyfriend, Levi, a homicide detective with the police department, does the same thing with me. I beg to differ. Maybe it's just that we're not as public about it.

Cole glanced toward the salon, hoping to catch a glimpse of his beloved, no doubt, but only got little ol' me. He smiled and waved. The elf handing out free cookies got a look at him and appeared frozen in a panic before she tossed the cup of cocoa she was handing to someone. She took off at a dead run toward the salon, tipping over the cookie table in the process. Frosted bells, trees, Santas, and angels scattered across the sidewalk. The elf glanced back at Cole as he chased her through the line of customers in front of the salon.

A customer coming in held the door wide open as she watched the spectacle unfold, giving me better access as well. Ms. Elf knocked over two people, a man and a woman.

"Hey!" the man boomed. "What's the meaning of this?"

"How dare you!" the woman yelled, unsure who she was mad at yet, the man who fell into her or the elf. Until she saw Cole coming toward the line. Her eyes bulged, and she rolled into a ball and covered her head. "I'm suing, dontcha know!" she said, her voice muffled through her arms.

The elf veered off toward the parking lot, and Cole followed. Whoever the elf was, she was light on her feet and rabbit-fast, having an advantage over Cole, who was in uniform with a duty belt.

"Stop!" Cole ordered. But the elf kept on going, effortlessly hopping over Santa's El Camino.

It was like watching something from a TV show, and all eyes were glued to the cop chasing the elf, making the free haircut customers forget their grumbling for a moment. Almost.

"Come on!" A woman shrieked. "I'm not missing my free haircut because you want to see this fiasco play out."

"Yeah," another piped up.

By this time, the ladies and their patrons stood in front of the window staring at the scene.

"Anyone got any popcorn?" the woman in the doorway asked. "This is quite the show."

Claire watched Cole in horror.

"Good grief," Claire exclaimed, "Cole is going to pull something. A hamstring or a calf muscle."

"Buy a nurse costume," Rubie said, grinning. "He'll wish he'd pulled something sooner."

I laughed. Connie's cheeks reddened like strawberries, and one side of Babs' lips turned up with amusement. Leave it to girly-girl Rubie to add to the entertainment.

"Come on, guys," I said. "This is like an impending train wreck none of us can stop watching, but we need to get crackilackin, or we really *will* be here until midnight."

"Not me," said Rubie. "Scott and I have plans." She led her client back to her chair. "Come on, Wilma."

Rubie dated so many men I'd lost count until she met Scott. He wasn't typical of the type she went out with, but he caught her attention and interest and held it. He worked with Levi and Cole at the police department. That's how they met. He tagged along with Levi and Cole to Grizzley's Tap House, our stomping ground, when they met Claire and me for dinner and drinks, and Rubie tagged along with us. None of us had any intention of setting them up. It just happened.

After all of the drama, which ended with the elf's escape and Cole back to providing security, the next two hours went seamlessly. Christmas music piped through the ceiling speakers, the white lights around our stations, the front desk, and the Christmas tree twinkled merrily, adding life to the place. The blue and white inflatable angel in the corner swayed each time the cold air blew in through the opened door. The customers came at the appropriate times, and we were like a well-oiled machine as we washed, cut, and blow-dried the hair of person after person. The deal was for a haircut, but without styling, only a quick blow dry, so we didn't send them out into the Minnesota frigid air with wet hair, sending someone to their death from cold or pneumonia.

As I checked out each client at the front counter, I surveyed the scene from the nearly-floor-to-ceiling windows. Everyone appeared to be having the time of their lives; kids ran and giggled, adults visited with each other. A family stood by Cole, the little boy on his father's shoulders, the mother holding a baby riding low on her hip, bundled up like the Stay Puft Marshmallow Man. I wished Cole would come fill us in on the elf debacle and why he chased her. The person supplying the cookies must have brought more out because children happily munched on them. Hopefully they weren't the ones from the ground.

Inside the walls of this cozy Christmas wonderland Claire and I had created, blow dryers hummed, people laughed, but it lacked the pungent, yet familiar and comforting, aroma of hair and nail chemicals. Within the first two hours, I think all of us appreciated more than ever performing these services. And I noticed that few of the customers so far were regular clientele. Although I hadn't known Patti was a regular either.

As I thought of Patti, I realized her turn should be coming up soon. I glanced over at the waiting corner and saw Trudy perched to one side of the tree, waiting patiently with a magazine open. I hoped Patti waited a bit longer so we wouldn't have another incident. As if feeling my attention on her, Trudy slapped her magazine down on the table and wrapped her scarf around her neck.

"I'm heading outside for a bit," she said to me. "I'll be back."

I nodded, acknowledging I heard her.

Besides our hair clientele, a steady stream of people came in to use the tanning booths and the restrooms. Thankfully, everything stayed orderly, much to my relief. After the rough start we had, I welcomed an orderly atmosphere. Speaking of restrooms, however, the line was getting longer.

As if reading my mind, Rubie brushed up beside me. "You should have listened when I told you not to let everyone come in and use the bathroom, chicklet."

"Chicklet?" I asked, shaking my head. She came up with the oddest pet names. "I'm trying to be customer friendly."

"Yeah, but it's not our customers using the bathroom. It's everyone else. I've been trying to get in for a good half hour now and haven't been able to. Pretty soon I'll be swimming there."

"Thanks for the visual," I said, grinning.

"Ma'am?" a girl in her early teens said. I bristled at the word. It's always been a term that's bothered me. Why, I have no idea, except it makes me feel old.

"Yes?" I asked, looking at her as I turned my stylist chair and pumped it up a notch with my foot. I turned my attention back to my client, made another *snip snip*, turned her chair slightly, and glanced back at the girl.

"That one bathroom has been occupied for a long time. People are coming in and out of one, but the other door has stayed locked."

Great. "If it's still occupied when I finish with this haircut, I'll check it out, okay? Give me about five minutes."

"Thank you, ma'am," she said, the picture of perfect politeness.

"Melanie," I said, smiling at her. "You can call me Melanie." She was the cutest little thing, and my heart melted.

The girl went to the back of the line, shifting her weight from one foot to the other. I hurried through the blow-dry to see what the hold-up was.

"Melanie," Claire said up at the desk as she was ringing up some Paul Mitchell product for her client, "if we do this next year, we need to rethink our decision to open the restrooms to the public."

"I totally agree. There are porta-potties in the parking lot." She wrinkled her nose. "I know they're gross. I wouldn't be caught dead in them. But there are facilities at the grocery store they can use. I can't imagine they wouldn't be open to the public."

I sent my client off with a thank you and one of my business cards and darted back to the restrooms where the teenaged girl had made little progress moving forward. She pointed to the occupied one, and I knocked. Nothing.

"Hello?" I said as I knocked again and put my ear to the door. Nothing. "Hello? I said louder and listened again. "If someone is in there, please let me

know, or I'm coming in." I put my ear to the door
again.

Babs brushed by me and turned into the office,
snagging her blue aluminum water bottle from the
desk. "I'll bet someone accidentally locked it when
they left. I'm surprised it hasn't happened before
this," she said.

I nodded and pursed my lips. "True story." I
stepped across the hall into the office, grabbed the key
from the top right-hand drawer, and then knocked
again for good measure before opening the door. It
met me with resistance. "What in the heck?" I
mumbled as I leaned into the door with my shoulder
and pushed it open. I gasped when I saw why it
wouldn't give. Lying on the floor behind the door was
Patti.

3

I placed two fingers on her carotid. No pulse. I felt her wrist as an extra precaution. Nothing.

"Claire!" I hollered over the buzz of blow dryers and the din of chatter and laughter. I pulled the door mostly closed, keeping it ajar with my foot. "My apologies," I said to the line of people, "but the restrooms are closed. You will have to use the porta-potties in the parking lot or head on down to the grocery store."

"Gross!" a few of them said at the same time. "Those porta-potties are disgusting!"

"As I said, if you don't want to use those, then head down to the grocery store. Please," I said as they tried my patience. The teenaged girl looked at me, eyes wide in desperation, and I motioned toward her with my head. "What's your name?"

"Jenny," she said, barely able to stop from dancing from foot to foot.

"Jenny," I said, "go ahead and take the other bathroom as soon as the person comes out."

"Hey!" Someone complained. "How come she gets to stay here? She's at the end of the line."

I narrowed my eyes and glared at the culprit, daring her to argue with me. "Because I own the place and told her she could."

I must have appeared threatening because she didn't say another word, just turned and sulked away.

The person in the available bathroom left, and Jenny bolted for it with another look of desperation. "Thank you so much, ma'am—Melanie," she said before yanking the door closed behind her.

Claire appeared around the corner. "What's going on?" she asked, her shears in one hand, a comb in the other.

I took my foot from the door and let it close. "Guard this door with your life. Don't let anyone in here. I'm going to run and get security."

"Why?" Her brows furrowed, but her smile stayed in place. A trick I've never been able to figure out.

"Don't freak out, but we have a dead body in there." I jerked my thumb toward the door.

"What?" she screeched.

So much for not freaking out, but who could blame her? Of course, she should be getting used to it by now.

"Stay right here, okay? Don't let anyone in this room. I'll explain further in a second." I turned and ran out of the short hallway, through the salon, and out the door.

A blast of cold air slapped my face, and I wrapped my arms around myself as I raced toward Cole who was chatting it up with a few of the festival-goers a few feet away from Santa's chair. Trudy was one of them. A little boy of maybe five was sitting on Santa's knee, his hands clasped in his lap as he talked.

"Birch Haven is not as small as it once was," one of the men said to Cole and proceeded to launch into another comment.

"Cole," I interrupted, tugging on his sleeve. "You need to come to the salon. Now!"

Cole zeroed in on me. "Is Claire okay?"

"Yes," I quickly assured him. "But Patti Parker isn't. She's on the restroom floor. Dead." I thought I'd said it rather quietly, but apparently not.

Trudy let out a sharp gasp, and her hand flew to her chest. "Oh, my God!" she exclaimed.

The next thing I knew, Santa jumped up, and a little boy slid off his knee and onto the floor. A woman, presumably the boy's mother, jumped up onto the platform and scooped up the child, cursing at Santa.

"Mommy!" the little boy cried. "You can't talk to Santa that way, or I won't get what I asked for!"

"He's a fake!" Another child yelled, pointing at Santa, who was now running toward the grocery store. "He's not Santa!"

"Mommy!" the dumped little boy cried. "Is that true?"

So much was happening at once that after calling in backup on his radio, Cole and I both stood rooted in place. Cole was likely deciding what fire he needed to put out first, and me because—well because just when I thought the day couldn't get any more bizarre than it had been earlier, it did.

Trudy stood unmoving until she glanced at me and sputtered, "I—I—I didn't do it! I did not kill that witch!"

Cole apparently decided the body was top priority because he trotted toward the salon. He snapped around to look at Trudy, pointed at her, and ordered, "You come with me until backup arrives."

"I will not," she argued. Her eyes sparked behind a wall of fear.

"Lady," he warned, but it was too late. She was gone.

"I've got her last name," I assured him.

"Write it down for me," he called over his shoulder as we turned into the salon.

Connie, Babs, and Rubie all stopped what they were doing and stared at us. Their clients followed suit.

"Lock the door," Cole ordered to no one in particular. "No one else comes in. And no one leaves."

This, of course, did nothing but startle people into panic mode. The customers sitting in the stylist and manicure chairs stood and grabbed their purses, unsure which way to go. The four people in the waiting area did the same. They couldn't decide whether they should flee toward the door or stay to find out what happened.

"What'd you do?" Rubie whispered, now standing right by my side.

My mouth flew open and my hand to my chest. "Why do you just automatically assume I did something?"

She tilted her head and raised an eyebrow. "Really?" she asked. Her tone dripped with skepticism.

"I didn't do anything!" I insisted before locking the front door. I turned toward the salon. "Just stay calm," I said as loudly as I could while trying to be calm myself. But I needed everyone to hear over the panicked questions, all firing at once.

"What's going on?"

"Why's the cop here?"

"Why can't we leave?"

"They can't keep us here!"

"Please!" I said louder.

"Is someone dead?" A man asked as he puffed out his chest with a territorial look. The tight short sleeves on his T-shirt revealed well-developed muscles and a sleeve of tattoos on one arm. "I can help."

"Are you a doctor?" I asked him with a glimmer of hope.

"No. Bouncer at a bar."

I exhaled my disappointment and shook my head. *Of course, you are.* "Thanks, but no thanks," I said. "Just have a seat, please."

"If someone among us is a killer," he said forcefully, "you'll need someone to take charge here."

I took a deep, calming breath before dealing with this bozo. "That's what the police are for," I said. "Besides, no one said anything about a killer."

"Well, no disrespect, lady, but I'm not taking chances. If there's a body, that means there's a killer. And I'm not—"

"A body doesn't mean it was a murder, you idiot," an elderly woman scolded him. "If I have a heart attack and die, it's not murder." She narrowed her eyes. "Unless you give me one. Now sit down like she told you, sonny. Got it?" She shook her bony finger at him.

I didn't know whether I was thankful for her or afraid of her. Evidently, the bouncer was afraid of her because he shut up and sat down without another word.

A woman came out of one of the three tanning booths. I had forgotten about the tanners! She had on a pair of Adidas jogging pants and a hoodie, a duffle bag slung over her shoulder. Her skin was darn near darker than Claire's from the artificial rays. I hated those darn booths and kept saying I would get rid of them, but it was one of those things I kept putting off. It's good business for the Minnesota winters when the sun goes into hiding more often than not. The tanner stopped in her tracks. Her gaze darted around the salon, the whites of her eyes looking even whiter against the tan.

"Um...what's going on?" she asked to no one in particular.

"Someone's dead in the bathroom," said the bouncer. Grandma shot him a look and pointed her finger at him. *Yikes! He was taking his life in his hands here.*

I glanced toward the hallway in the back corner of the salon, wishing backup would get there so I could leave my post. As if on cue, someone jerked on the door then pounded twice on the glass. I spun around to see Levi, his gloved fingers curled around the handle. Two more police cars pulled into the parking lot, followed by a fire truck.

"I don't know about you, Blondie," Levi said the minute I opened the door.

Levi and I met a couple of years ago over another dead body in my salon. That one died in my stylist chair, so I was, of course, a suspect. After the case was over and they cleared me, he asked me out. And after I resisted—until I couldn't anymore—for no other reason than fear of losing my independence, we became what Sydney calls *a thing*. Between then and now, he's grown used to the fact that I tend to get into trouble. But in my defense, he credits much to me that I've had nothing to do with. Like this.

"I didn't do anything!" I said as I followed on his heels. Another burst of cold air blew through the salon as the backup officers came in the door. I heard one of them address the salon patrons, instructing who they wanted where. I silently wished them good luck with Grandma and Sonny.

Levi squeezed in between Cole and the body while Claire watched from behind. I slid in beside Claire to hear Levi and Cole's conversation but stayed quiet, not wanting to draw attention to our presence and risk him asking us to move. I peeked around the corner into the salon. Babs and Rubie worked furiously to finish up their clients to get the scoop on what was going on. Rubie's gaze met mine with a question mark. Connie appeared to be taking her time, in contrast to the other two. From what I knew of Connie, she'd be just fine sticking her head in the sand in delightful ignorance. Given that she liked to keep things simple and crime-free, it's a wonder she has stuck it out at the salon since we'd opened.

"Why didn't you call 911?" Claire whispered.

"The first thing I thought of was Cole since he was right outside the place."

"Your grandmother is never going to believe this," she said.

"She doesn't have to know."

"Yeah, right. There are two things wrong with that theory. One, you can't keep a secret from her. And, two, she can read you like a book she's memorized."

Levi turned toward us. "The two of you need to leave, please."

35

"Where would you like us to go?" I asked, raising my eyebrows. "It's our salon."

"It's my crime scene," he countered.

"In *our* salon," I argued.

He exhaled slowly and dropped his head a moment before shaking it slightly. "You're going to kill me one of these days."

"I'm just saying—"

"Please," he said, his eyes meeting mine, pleading.

"I'm not about to go back out there." I jerked my thumb toward the salon area. "It's more brutal out there than in the cold outside."

"Then go outside," he said. "Problem solved."

I took hold of Claire's arm. "We'll go to the office."

He dropped his chin and stared at me. "Right next to the room in which we're working? What are the chances?"

I shrugged and smiled sheepishly. He knew what I was up to, so trying to tell him otherwise was useless.

Claire and I crossed the hall and into the office in three steps. Or rather, I took three steps. Claire's long legs carried her in one. Levi closed the door as much as possible.

"Why do you insist on giving the poor guy such a hard time?" Claire asked, still watching Levi and Cole through the door that was cracked open.

"Keeps him on his toes," I said, my gaze glued to him so as not to miss a thing he did. "Now quiet, so I can hear what they're saying."

"Nosy Nellie," she said, chuckling.

"Shh!"

Levi turned and looked at me over the rim of his glasses. He wore them infrequently, but he appeared incredibly sexy in them.

"What?" I asked, lifting my hands, palms skyward.

I swear his lip quivered before he turned away from me as he tried not to smile.

4

"Melanie—" Claire started.

"Shh," I said again, resting my finger against my lips.

Rubie turned the corner into the office, nearly knocking me over. She stifled a scream when she caught a glimpse of the body and then turned toward me, eyes narrowed. "You did do something. I knew it!"

"I did not!" I said, a tad defensively. "And I would appreciate it if you could keep it zipped so I can hear what's going on."

"Feel free to continue talking up a storm, Rubie," Levi said without missing a beat in his investigation.

"All of you are impossible," I said. "Impossible!"

A frumpy man, needing to tighten his belt a few notches and with a comb-over that was every stylist's nightmare (revealing more scalp than hair), came around the corner. Levi glanced at him and nodded toward me.

"Melanie," Levi said, "meet CSI Sanders. Sanders, Melanie Hogan. Co-owner of the crime scene."

"Hey!" I protested. "That wasn't nice." I scowled.

Sanders snickered. "No worries, ma'am. I'm familiar with Wescott's dismal attempt at humor. Besides, I know you're his gal. Everyone knows it."

I raised my eyebrows at Levi who smirked. "Gal?" I mouthed. Who says *gal* anymore these days?

Claire and Rubie talked amongst themselves, Claire filling in Rubie on what transpired. I took a step into the hallway so their chatter didn't drown out Levi and Sanders. Levi looked at me and shook his head, but he didn't say a word. Saving his energy, no doubt.

I watched as Levi issued instructions and Sanders obliged, bagging a half-empty diet soda bottle — probably the one Claire asked her not to open. Next they examined and bagged an empty Dixie coffee cup, the kind which we keep by our coffee maker in the salon. Patti's arm lay in the coffee, her sleeve soaking up the dark liquid.

"Is that a pill?" I blurted, pointing over Levi's shoulder and toward Pattie's outstretched hand. He was squatted beside Patti's left side. Sanders hunched over him, taking in my find.

"Looks like it," Sanders said.

"That's great!" I exclaimed. "So we might just be looking at an overdose, right?"

Levi stopped and pivoted on the ball of his right foot to look at me, nearly knocking over Sanders. "*We*? And for God's sake, Sanders, take a step back," he growled.

Sanders, unfazed by Levi's demand, stood, took a step back, and swiped a hand over his comb-over, pushing the sparse strands back. "Sure thing, Wescott."

"Yeah, *we*," I said to Levi. "I don't want another murder in my salon. It's bad enough to have two deaths, but both murders? Come on!" I shuddered.

Levi took a tweezer out of his bag and picked up the little green pill, studying it before dropping it into a baggie. "Looks like Oxy," he said to Sanders. And to me — unintentionally.

"So it could have been an overdose, right?" I asked, hopeful.

"Anything's possible." He picked up Patti's hand and inspected her nail beds, then her eyes.

A woman clad in navy waterproof winter wear, a county medical examiner emblem on her coat, turned the corner. A younger man that was with her held back.

"I'll wait here," he said, and she answered with a curt nod.

Thank goodness. There were already too many people crammed in this small space. One more caused a bit of claustrophobia.

She stripped off her coat and handed it to me without a glance before she slipped on a pair of latex gloves. I'm not sure what I was expecting from a medical examiner, but it wasn't her. She was brusque and impersonal with blood-shot eyes and unruly hair escaping from her ponytail holder. I shrugged and lay her coat over the back of the chair before quickly getting back to the door so I could hear better.

"What have we got?" she asked Levi who watched as Sanders took additional photographs of Patti's hands and face.

"White female—"

"You done with the body?" she asked, not waiting for him to finish.

I thought about bumping her coat to the floor but didn't want to move from my spot for fear of missing what they said.

"Yup," he answered.

She weaseled her way in closer. She felt Patti's wrist, lay two fingers against her carotid, and said in a brusque manner, "Deceased." She glanced at her watch.

"No kidding," I mumbled, unaware I'd spoken the words out loud until she glanced at me sharply. Levi looked at me, eyebrows raised. I quickly averted my gaze down and away. "Sorry," I muttered.

She went back to her work, cold as the weather outside and completely disinterested. Just another day on the job. I thought it sad that a person could get to that degree of detachment from a dead body. That being said, I wasn't too horrified here, which says far too much of what my past couple of years have been like.

Levi took off one glove, then the second, folding one into the other, before tossing them into the trashcan. He extracted a clean pair from his bag and slipped them on as he stepped into the hallway.

Ms. Rude Examiner rested one hand on her knee, the other on the wall, and pushed herself to a standing position with an audible grunt. "Man, this age thing is hell," she complained. She snagged a mini recorder from her fanny pack, clicked a button and said, "Time of death between one and one-thirty. Cause of death unknown until an autopsy is performed. Foul play not ruled out."

"Wait!" I blurted. "Foul play?" So much for my overdose theory. My eyes darted around the small restroom, taking in the strewn contents of Patti's purse.

The M.E. turned to look at me without the slightest bit of interest. Not even irritation for interrupting her.

"Can't rule anything out at this point. Not until I perform the autopsy." Her tone held no emotion. She then continued talking into her recorder.

My pulse ticked up a notch and my blood roared in my eardrums. *Could this be murder? But who?*

I stepped into the hallway and scanned the salon. Other than three officers in addition to Cole, Rubie, Connie, and Babs, the salon was now empty. The young man who arrived with the M.E. remained on the perimeter of the scene, thumbs hooked through his belt loops. A large group of people plastered their faces against the floor-to-ceiling glass wall that ran along the front of the salon. Some had their hands cupped around their faces to see better. It was all like something out of a murder mystery novel. Except this is what my life had become. Sadly, I'd come to expect a dead body to show up in my world. On the bright side, I'd become a pretty darn good detective, much to Levi's dismay. But given that I'd helped him solve a crime on more than one occasion, I hoped he'd one day appreciate my expertise. Even though I've never been witness to a miracle, I know they've happened before.

Moments later, the officers blocked the hallway as best they could from the prying eyes on the other side of the glass as Levi, the medical examiner, and her assistant loaded the body on the gurney. After covering her with a sheet, they wheeled her out the door. The police officers marched on either side, blocking the looky-loos as best they could.

The coroner's van pulled away and the officers came back in to talk with the ladies. I knew I was next, as was Claire. At least this time they couldn't blame me. I'd had nothing to do with Patti, and when I found the body, I hadn't been alone with her. Jenny came to mind, the young teenaged girl who alerted me to the locked door. *Could she?* "No!" I answered myself quickly.

"No, what?" Levi asked.

"Nothing. Just running things through my mind. You know, possibilities."

"How about you tell me what you were thinking just now and I'll decide if it's a no or not."

"There was a girl, early teens, who let me know that the bathroom had been occupied for so long. That's how I knew to check it out."

"What makes you think she is connected?"

"I don't. That's why you heard me say *no*."

"Melanie," he said, taking a slow breath, "there must be a reason you thought about her at all."

I shrugged then shook my head. I remembered the guy who stated that she'd been at the end of the line. "No, not really. Just that she's the one who told me about the locked door. She was at the end of the line so she couldn't have been here long enough to know the room had been occupied that long," I said. "So she might have been—"

"How long had she been in line?" he asked.

I shrugged and frowned. "How would I know that? I was cutting hair, not keeping tabs on people in the potty line."

He held a hand up then pressed a fist against his lips. "The potty line," he said, struggling to conceal a smile. He took a minute then said, "Do you know her last name? Was she on the waiting list? For the haircut line, not the potty line," he added and smirked.

"We just had a possible murder in here and you're amused?" I asked, my hands on my hips.

"At you, not the murder. There's a difference."

"Happy to be of service." I took a deep breath, tipped my head back and looked skyward before I went to the front desk to search the list of names. "No Jenny." I strode back to the hallway.

"Maybe she wasn't a customer," Claire said. "I bet over half of the people in line weren't." She looked at Levi with serious eyes. "The potty line."

I bit my cheek and pressed my lips together to stop a witty remark. I turned toward the window. Since the body had been taken away, all of the looky-loos had disappeared. I shook my head. "Not that I'm disappointed they're all gone," I said, flinging my arm toward the window, "but what is it about death and mayhem that people are drawn to?"

"Especially holiday mayhem," Rubie said.

I jumped and snapped my head around to look at her. *Geez!* I'd been so wrapped up in the events I'd forgotten she was even here. Connie and Babs, too.

"Gentleman?" Levi called to the officers without looking up from the notepad he scribbled something on. "Everything good out there?"

"Yes, sir," said Officer Johnson. His frame suddenly filled the doorway. "We'll interview the ladies out there." He jerked his thumb toward the salon. "And then we'll be back for you two," he said, pointing toward me and Claire.

"Oh, joy," I said, rolling my eyes. Levi looked at me over the rim of his glasses. "What?" I said. "It's not like I haven't been through this too many times already. I could tell them what questions to ask me."

47

"I can't interview Claire," Cole said to Officer Johnson, "so I'll interview one of the others and you talk with Claire."

Johnson shrugged a shoulder. "Okay. Ms. Davis," he said, holding up a pen, "let's talk over here." He led the way toward the waiting area.

Officer Clark said to me, "I'll be with you in a bit."

"You know where I'll be," I said. Levi, investigating the rest of the scene with Sanders now that the body was gone, turned toward me. "I'll be in the office. Geez!" I said, hands up, palms facing him. "You're so territorial. And in *my* territory."

Cole was talking with Connie when his pen stopped mid-stroke at something she said. I couldn't tell if it was the glare from the white lights against his already light skin or if he paled at what Connie said. Color began creeping up his neck and he scraped a hand through his short military cut. My heart ticked up a notch. That couldn't be good.

My stomach fluttered, and I forced myself to go into the office, glancing in the restroom as I did. Levi was examining another pill between his latex-gloved thumb and forefinger as Sanders looked on. It appeared the same size as the green one but was white in color. He scribbled something more on his notepad.

"Wescott?"

Officer Anderson came into the hallway. I took a step back further into the office and around the corner so I could listen without Levi knowing.

"What?" Levi said.

"Sir, this might not be anything," he cleared his throat, "but Ms. Parker—"

"Rubie?" Levi asked.

"Yeah. Rubie. She said Ms. Davis—Claire is the one who brought the vic to the bathroom to clean up after a fight she was in outside. She—Claire—is the one who gave her the coffee, sir."

My mouth flew open, and I went completely still.

"Why would she bring coffee into the restroom?" Levi murmured, sounding like he was talking to himself and not Officer Anderson.

"Maybe she wanted it to swallow that pill you're holding there," Anderson said.

"She had a diet soda for that," Levi said.

"Like I said, it might be nothing," Anderson said. "Just thought you should know."

I felt a sick weight in the pit of my stomach. If this turned out to be murder, it wasn't looking good for Claire. Is that what Cole looked upset about? Did Connie tell him? But why hadn't he said anything? *Why would he, you dummy?* I scolded myself.

I stepped into the hallway and poked my head around the corner into the salon. As Connie talked, Cole looked toward me with furrowed brows.

"Mahoney!" Levi boomed.

Cole excused himself from Connie and came to the back hallway. "Yeah?"

"You're officially taken off this case as of now."

"Sir?" Cole asked, his tone now that of a subordinate rather than that of best friend.

"You're off. Anderson just found out that Claire is the one who gave the victim this cup of coffee that ended up on the floor here. If we find out the victim didn't die of natural causes, which I don't believe she did, Claire could have just become a suspect."

My stomach lurched and bitterness crept into my throat.

Levi's voice was hard, but so quiet I struggled to hear what he said. I took a step closer and could see Cole, his back stiff. His face burned red, including the tips of his ears. His high-fade flat top haircut wasn't his friend right now. The red was creeping up his neck again. "You can't honestly believe Claire would do this." His voice was as tight as the spot he'd found himself in.

"Of course not. But you know as well as I do, Mahoney, that the Chief isn't gonna give two craps about what I think. We have to play this one careful." I could tell Levi was working hard at trying to be both Cole's superior and his best friend, but the two were in obvious conflict right now. I hurt for both of them.

"I can clear her," Cole said, scraping through his hair with his hand again.

"No," Levi said, his tone firm. "No, you can't. The process will clear her, Cole. We always tell people to trust the process. Now it's your turn to do as we say."

I watched Cole, uncomfortable for him. His Adam's apple moved up and down as he swallowed hard.

"I'll let her know."

"No, you won't," Levi said, his voice a little softer. He stood and put his hand on Cole's shoulder. "Anderson will take it from here."

5

By the time all of the police presence left, it was a little after five. Connie, Babs, Rubie, Claire, and I each dropped into a chair in the salon.

"I don't know about you guys," Connie said, "but I'm ready to call it a day. Heck, I want to call it a week." Her voluptuous frame sank into the chair cushion, and she swiped her arm across her brow.

"Tell ya what," I said, "take tomorrow off. Heck, take the next day off, too. You've earned it."

Since tomorrow was Sunday and the salon is closed Sunday and Monday, I thought my offer would help lighten the mood a tad, but not a soul lifted. Mine either.

"Sorry," I mumbled into heavy silence that threatened to suffocate. And I usually like silence.

I looked at each of the ladies. Claire stared off into the darkening sky outside, her normally present smile tucked away somewhere. I hoped it would resurface soon. For that to happen, I needed to be sure she wasn't considered a suspect.

Connie stayed still as could be, her head resting against the back of the chair. I couldn't even be sure she was blinking. Babs, her tiny, lithe frame sitting straight up, studied one of her numerous tattoos on her right forearm. Between tattoos and piercings, she was a highly decorated nail tech. Her short, spiked hair fit her to a T, showing off perfect cheekbone structure and piercing blue eyes. And Rubie, usually a talking ball of energy, sat completely still. Her Norwegian descent gave her naturally light skin, but right now, she was merely pale.

I nudged her with the toe of my boot. "Hey, you okay?"

She met my eyes and shook her head. "No. I feel terrible. I think I'm gonna be sick." Her hand went to her stomach.

I sat up ramrod straight, and my eyes darted to the trash can as I contemplated moving it in front of her. "Sick from what?"

Rubie waved her hand at me. "Not that kind of sick," she said. She looked at Claire. "I am so sorry."

"For what?" Claire reached up and swiped off her green with red holly berries headscarf.

Claire had wild hair, and she usually tamed it with brightly colored scarves, worn in a dozen different ways. She's crazy creative. And crazy beautiful. But now her gorgeous chestnut skin appeared a bit peaked. Her eyes, usually sparkling brown pools with emerald specks, were dull. The only thing sparkling in the entire salon this evening were the white Christmas lights dancing in the darkening room. The sun had almost set, and the people in the parking lot had dispersed, leaving an eerie feeling. I half expected Patti to pull some kind of after-death stunt. I shivered and crossed my arms in front of me, rubbing my hands against my biceps.

"I didn't mean to get you into trouble," Rubie said to Claire. "He wanted me to walk him through the hours of noon and two—what I did, what I saw. It didn't occur to me that—"

"Rubie," Claire interrupted, "you have nothing to be sorry for. You did nothing wrong." She forced a smile as she leaned forward, her arms resting on her knees. "And neither did I. I know that."

"We all know that," Rubie said. "You would be the last one to hurt anyone or anything—living or not."

"True that," I said, smiling at Claire. She wouldn't even kill a spider but instead insisted on setting it free. And if she saw a dead animal on the road, rodent or otherwise? Well, one would hope she hadn't applied mascara yet. She had the most generous, giving spirit of anyone I knew. Except for my grandmother. I shook my head. "They aren't even a hundred percent sure that it is murder," I said. "And if it is, we'll get you cleared. I will make sure of it."

Claire groaned and rolled her eyes. She even chuckled. It was a sad, pathetic chuckle, but I'd take it. "You, my dear bestie, need to stay out of it," she said. "Please. I'm begging you."

"If it comes to that, I'm not going to just sit back and do nothing. Come on. You know me."

"Unfortunately, I do," she said and sat back again. But a trace of a smile was there, and if I didn't know better, she was relieved.

"I hate to be a downer on this party," Babs said, her hands clasped in front of her, her elbows resting on the armrests, "but they sounded pretty certain it wasn't a natural death. I don't know how they know that," she added, "but they sound confident if you ask me."

"She had a small rash on her cheeks and petechia in the whites of her eyes. It was small, but it was there. That happens when someone can't breathe," I said.

"So someone was in there and suffocated her?" Babs asked.

"That's not the only way," I said. "Certain drug reactions or poison could cause that, too. Or so I learned in one of the mystery novels I've read, anyway."

"It's a little unnerving that you know all of this," Rubie said, her brows furrowed.

"I was using my time wisely while I waited in the office," I said, studying my fingernails. "Don't let anyone tell you multitasking isn't healthy."

"You mean you were listening in on a conversation not meant for you," she corrected. "That's called being nosy."

"In some circles, yes."

"It's called being nosy, Mel," she insisted. She put her hands up, palms facing forward. "I'm not saying it's bad. I'm just calling it what it is."

I nodded and conceded. "Yeah, it's nosy. But I wanted to know what happened in our salon. For all of our sakes." Claire snickered, and it was so unexpected, it caught me off guard. "You okay?" I asked. "I mean under the—"

"Who would have thought this day would have spiraled to where it did? I mean, the whole afternoon, before we even opened our doors, was nothing short of bizarre." She snickered again, light returning to her eyes.

"Right?" I exclaimed. "When I saw the two women sparring in line before we'd even opened, I wondered what the afternoon would bring."

"When the elf took off running, it should have been a sign for us to close up shop right then and there," Claire said.

"Even more so when Santa took off running," I said. "I wonder if they've even found him yet?" I pondered the question before asking another. "Do you know why Cole chased the elf to begin with?" She shook her head. "Dang! I'd completely forgotten to ask him about that. What with the dead body and all." My thoughts were like jumping beans, bouncing all over the place. "Can you get him on the phone for me?"

She snatched her phone from the counter and punched a number. After her mushy greeting, followed by "Mel has a question for you," she thrust the phone toward me.

"Hey, Cole. Just curious about something," I started.

"You know what they say about curiosity," he said, his voice flat.

"Yeah, yeah, it killed the cat. What made you chase the elf?" As soon as the words were out of my mouth, I let out a misplaced chuckle. It sounded like I was reciting a nursery rhyme.

"She yelled some mumbo-jumbo about there's no way she's going to jail now," he said. "I thought she was a shoplifter or a pickpocket."

"Murderer?"

"Ask Levi," he said.

I winced at the tone of betrayal and shot up a quick prayer that this whole event wouldn't affect their friendship. "Thanks." I handed the phone back to Claire. When she hung up I said, "I'm going to call the company who hires out Santa to —"

Ruby gasped and her hand flew to her mouth. "You mean he's not real?"

I tossed a towel from my stylist station in her direction. It fell short and landed on the floor in front of her. "Before I was so rudely interrupted," I narrowed my eyes at her, "I'm going to call the Santa company to see who it was. It can't be a coincidence that he took off as soon as I told Cole that Patti was dead."

"Isn't that kind of a stretch to think he heard you?" Connie asked. "Were you that close to him?"

"Cole was standing within a few feet of the stage where Santa was sitting. A little boy was even sitting on his knee and slid to the ground when Santa stood and ran. Stunned the poor kid. Didn't know if he should cry or what."

"Huh," Babs said, processing the scene in her head. "While you're at it," she said, "find out if the same company hires the elves. Santa and the elf could be working together. On the set and off, so to speak."

I nodded. "Good point." We fell quiet again. The sun had now set, blanketing the salon in darkness except for the Christmas lights and the parking lot lights' dim glow. "Hey," I spoke into the silence, "do any of you know the young teenager that told me about the locked bathroom? Her name was Jenny. Anyone cut her hair?"

"Nope."

"Not me."

"Never saw her before."

"None of my clients were kids, and no Jenny."

They all said at the same time.

"I didn't see her name on the list," I said.

"Maybe she was just here to use the biff," Babs said.

I shrugged. "Maybe."

"You don't sound convinced," Rubie said.

"Do you really think a young kid—"

"She was a teen, not a young kid."

"Regardless, do you think someone that age would do something as serious as kill someone?" Rubie asked.

"Oh dear friend, you're so naïve sometimes. You don't watch the news, do you?" I said.

She shook her head. "Nope. It's depressing."

"I don't watch it either," I admitted. "But I skim the paper online every morning. Kids can do some pretty horrendous things."

"I don't even know what she looks like," Rubie said.

"Me either. I wasn't paying attention," Babs said.

"I'll keep an eye out for her," I said. "I described her to Levi."

I glimpsed my smartwatch and jumped up, heading toward the office to grab my stuff. "I have to go. I'm making Christmas cookies with my grandmother tomorrow. I need to stop by her house tonight to make sure we have everything and make a list of what we still need so I can pick it up tomorrow on my way to her house."

"Hey!" Rubie called from behind me. I turned. "What are we going to do about the people on the list who didn't get in because of the...well...you know...the —"

"The death?" I asked.

"Well, yeah," she stammered. "I didn't know what to call it since we don't know what happened. Those people shouldn't miss out because of something that wasn't their fault."

"How do we know one of them wasn't at fault?" I asked, raising an eyebrow.

"I'm serious," she said.

Connie and Babs had started getting their things together but now stopped to listen.

"She has a point," Claire said. "We should try to work them in. We have their contact info from the sign-in sheet. At least their phone numbers."

I scampered to the front desk and studied next week's schedule. "I don't know when we could. We're swamped. Christmastime is our busiest ever. Unless…" I trailed off, mentally running through my schedule for the next two days.

"Unless what?" Babs asked.

"Tomorrow I can't because I'm not going to cancel on my grandmother, but what do you guys think about opening Monday afternoon? We could divvy up the names and call to schedule a time for them to come in."

"Works for me," Babs said. "I think there are only like six people left for manicures."

"Only?" I said. "That's a lot to fit in for an afternoon."

"I only got in a couple before we had to close. Besides, you underestimate me." Babs grinned.

"Everyone else in?" I asked.

After I had a unanimous vote, I pored over the sign-in sheet for haircuts. I tore the paper into four different pieces.

"Whoever has the manicures on their list text their name and number to Babs," I said.

"I better not get little kids on mine," Rubie said. "I had a little boy spit on me today. It was so gross!"

"Why did he spit on you?" Connie asked, pretending to gag.

"Cause he didn't want his hair cut. The little monster. That is why I never want kids."

I felt a pang in my gut. I'm not able to have kids, and it's why my ex-husband left me, getting another woman knocked up and engaged before the ink was dry on our divorce papers. I had always held onto some hope that a miracle would happen and I would have a child. That hope had begun to fade to nearly nothing in the past year. But odd as it was, the past year is when I finally began finding peace with it.

I startled at a hand on my shoulder. I turned to see Rubie, looking like she was going to start crying.

"Melanie, I'm so sorry," she whispered. "I've got such a big mouth. That's twice in one day I've said something I shouldn't have."

I patted her hand. "Please don't worry about it, Rubie. I'm good."

She slid in for a side hug. "Love you," she said.

"Love you, too, kid. Now scoot," I said. "See you all Monday at about noon."

6

Before I left the salon, I called Nana to let her know I would be there in just a few minutes. I knew she would have dinner ready, and I didn't want her to wait for me to get there before eating. Though I figured she would anyway. As luck would have it, she compiled the ingredient inventory that day and named off a handful of items for me to pick up. In all honesty, she didn't need my help for that to begin with. She was the master chef and baker, and I was the continuing education student.

Nana has been teaching me to cook for years. Though I had mastered it well enough to feel confident that I wouldn't starve, we still had lessons whenever possible. Time in her kitchen has always been priceless for both of us. It's when we really connected, solving the world's problems, talking about our day, our thoughts, our dreams, and sometimes about the townsfolk. To be fair, I sometimes talked about the townsfolk, but Nana didn't. I've never heard Nana say an unkind word about anyone. Ever.

Nana was my hero and mentor in life. Violet, my birth mother, decided she wanted to be a big movie star when I was four and left for California, leaving me with Nana and Granddad. Though I've fought abandonment issues because of that — and deep resentment toward Violet — I had the best, most stable upbringing a girl could ever hope for. A home filled with love and laughter and good food. And since Nana had been a nurse back then, I received the best medical attention for scraped knees and wounded feelings. But I'd always secretly wondered what I'd done to deserve to be dropped off on a doorstep by my birth mother, like I was a sack of trash, for someone else to raise. To add insult to injury, Violet never did make it in the movie industry; she only made it into a heap of trouble. Trouble for which she's still paying. And yet she never came back for me. A blessing to be sure, but it still hurt.

As soon as I hung up with Nana, I trotted down to the grocery store at the end of the mall, snagged a hand-held shopping basket, and began my journey. Finding what I needed always proved to be a treasure hunt unless it involved the frozen section for a quick microwave meal or the bakery. I think our salon alone funded the bakery.

I headed there first, and Stormi Wilson, baker extraordinaire and friend, was busily cruising around the area behind the counter. I chuckled at the reindeer antler headband adorned with blinking lights atop her head. I watched as she flitted between shelves until she spotted me and grinned before jogging to the front counter.

When she was close enough to hear, I pointed to the antlers and said, "Love the holiday spirit you got going on there."

She flashed a broad grin and touched them. "Me, too! Whatcha up to?" She wiped her hands on a towel and tucked it into her waistband.

"I should ask you the same thing," I said. "I'd have thought you'd be long gone by now."

"Knew you were comin' in and stayed just for you," she said with a wink. "Nah, I needed to check my dough situation so I can make some caramel rolls when I get in tomorrow morning."

"Your morning is middle of the night for me," I said. "Don't let me keep you. I'm sure you need to get home so you can get to bed. I'm just here to grab some goodies to bring to my grandmother's tomorrow. We're baking Christmas cookies all day."

She frowned and came around the counter to stand beside me. "No offense, but if you're baking all day, why in the h-e-double-l do you need to buy baked goods from me? Your baking can't be *that* bad."

She watched me as if waiting for me to admit something horrendous.

I waved my hand. "Well, Nana's isn't, but mine...well, that's another story."

Stormi laughed and touched my shoulder. "Oh, you! You're teasing me."

"Umm...not really." I chuckled. "When are you planning to open your own place?" I asked as I opened an acrylic door on one of the display cases. I reached for the tongs and a paper sack. I grabbed hold of a bear claw for Nana, and then a blueberry cream cheese-filled croissant for me.

"You know those aren't fresh, right?"

"Of course," I said. "They'll be even less so tomorrow, but they'll still be good. Our stuff won't be done until the afternoon. We need something to start the day off with our coffee."

"From what I know of your grandmother, she'll have something ready and offended that you brought commercial goodies."

I shrugged as I sealed up the bag. "More for me then."

"Hey," she said in a loud whisper as she slid in next to me. "What happened down at your end this afternoon? You sure had the police presence goin' on. Not to mention the entire population for the

Christmas Festival." Her eyes, deep brown, peered down at me.

"Gosh, where to even start." I shifted my weight from one foot to the other and glanced at my watch.

"Just the basics. What caused the commotion?"

"Someone died in the restroom at the salon," I whispered.

She gasped, and her hand flew to her chest. "Oh, my God! Again?" she shrieked.

"Shh!" I put my finger against my lips and skimmed the area to see how much attention we were holding. Only a few people turned to look before going back about their merry business. Apparently, it wasn't as loud as I'd thought. Maybe I was just still on edge. "I'm telling you, Stormi, Claire and I have had the worst luck." I kept mum about Claire being a potential suspect.

"Who was it?" she asked, looking rattled. "Anyone I would know?"

I shrugged a shoulder. "It was one of Claire's clients."

"Poor Claire," she said. "She must be devastated."

You have no idea. "Yeah, she is."

"And so soon after one of your own clients died. But look at it this way, at least this one wasn't murder." I stayed quiet and averted my gaze briefly before looking back at her. Her hand covered her mouth. "No!" she exclaimed.

"It's too soon to tell. All I know is I need to get the rest of my things and on to my grandmother's house. Over the river and through the woods, to grandmother's house I go."

She gave me a pathetic half-smile and reached over for a side hug. "Dang, girl. Birch Haven PD is going to have to hire another officer just for you. You hang in there, okay?" she said. "And if you guys need anything, just say the word." She shook her head slowly.

"Thanks, Stormi. Hey, you have a good evening. Save one of those caramel rolls for me."

She waved a hand in dismissal and lifted her chin slightly. "I'll bake you fresh ones Tuesday morning."

"Deal," I said with a last wave.

***

When I pulled into my grandmother's driveway, it was nearly seven o'clock. I hoped she heeded my advice and ate without waiting for me. The light above the kitchen sink was on and the flicker of the television shone through the living room window where the curtains didn't quite meet. Watching the news, no doubt. Or her favorite *Golden Girls* reruns. I enjoyed ribbing her about how she was just like Sophia. Every time she laughed and said the same thing: *You betcha!* In reality, however, Nana is nothing like Sophia at all. In fact, the opposite. Nana has long, beautiful silver hair she usually wears in a single loose braid. She's strong and so smart, but on the quiet side. And she always has a way of looking peaceful yet a little mischievous with her twinkling periwinkle-colored eyes.

I smiled at the vision of her in my head, grabbed the bags from the passenger seat, and opened my door. The cold slapped my cheeks, and a dog barked from the neighbor's yard. Nana's fat cat jumped up into the window between the curtains and perched on her ledge. "How you can fit on that ledge is beyond me, Callie Cat," I muttered and shook my head. I teased Nana that she had to quit feeding that cat so much, but Nana showed love through food. I would know. She was always telling me I need to eat more, put some weight on my bones, and often had a plate of food on the table for me before I could even take my coat off.

I opened the door and called out, "Nana, I'm here!" The smell of something spicy and delicious made my stomach grumble. I hadn't realized I was hungry until now.

She turned the corner, and my heart warmed. She was tucked into her fuzzy blue robe, her braid hanging over her shoulder. I set my bags down and enveloped her in a hug.

"Hello, dear," she said, gripping me tight. For a woman of her small stature and her age, she was strong. And feisty. And I loved that about her. I learned from the best. Except she had much better control of her tongue than I did. I had a little to learn in that department and have come to terms with the fact that it might never happen.

"It smells delightful in here!" I pulled away, holding her hands in mine, and looked into her eyes. "Please tell me you ate and didn't wait for me."

Her eyes sparkled with merriment. "I did, dear. But I have a plate ready just to warm up for you. Come," she said, leading me by the hand from the enclosed breezeway and into the kitchen. "I'll sit with you. I want to hear all about your day."

My stomach turned. That's the last thing I wanted to talk about and the last thing I wanted to worry her with.

"How about we talk about *your* day," I offered. "I always love to hear what kind of trouble you've gotten into," I razzed.

She chuckled. "Oh, just the usual, dontcha know."

Transplants to Minnesota tease us about our dialect and assume we all talk like the characters straight from the movie *Fargo*. We tend to think we're the ones who speak 'normal,' and others have an accent.

She busied herself with taking a plate from the fridge and refastening the plastic wrap.

"Geez, Nana! Who do you think is going to eat all that?"

"Well, you, dear," she said. "You need to — "

"Put some meat on those bones," I finished, trying to sound just like her. "But if I eat all that, I'll have to buy a whole new wardrobe five sizes bigger." Buying a new wardrobe wouldn't be a bad thing for most women. But there are a million and one things I'd rather do than shop. Even going to the dentist if I needed to choose between the two.

Nana laughed softly. "Oh, the drama, little one."

"Truth." I grabbed the grocery bags from the table in the breezeway and brought them into the kitchen.

"What's that one?" she asked, pointing to the bakery sack.

"A treat for tomorrow morning. If we're starting early, we'll need energy. Stormi says hi."

"Sweet gal, that one. But not like my Claire." She beamed. "God broke the mold after making that one."

"Hey!" I said, my eyes narrowed, and my jaw opened.

She came over and pinched my cheeks gently, leaning in close to my face. "You know you're my number one girl."

I smiled, pacified. When Claire says Nana spoils me, she's not lying. I was never a difficult child, but that doesn't mean I was easy, either. Nana and Granddad were saints. Nana still is.

I started taking things out of the bags and set them on the countertop. I picked up a bag of butterscotch chips she had among her things.

"Yum! Can I open these?"

She turned to look at what I was referring to. "After dinner."

"You run a tight ship, Mrs. Donnelly." I tossed the bag back onto the counter.

She smiled. When she and Claire were in the same room together, I had on more than one occasion counted how many times each smiled and kept a running tally in my head. Between the two of them, they've got the entire town beat.

"So tell me about your day," she said, sliding a steaming plate of meatloaf, green beans, and cornbread in front of me.

"Grab a fork," I said, looking at the plate.

"There's one right beside you."

"I meant for you. There's no way I can eat all of this, Nana."

"Eat what you can," she said and sat down caddy-corner from me. "Now quit stalling and tell me about your day." She rested an elbow on the table, her chin in her hand, and studied me. "You're procrastinating."

I looked at her and hesitated, then exhaled slowly. I pushed my plate away about an inch, and she pushed it back toward me about two inches, not missing a beat. "Talk, child. You're sending me into a fit."

"Someone died in the salon," I blurted and shoveled a bit of meatloaf in my mouth.

"Oh, dear," she said, covering my left hand with hers. She didn't, however, sound surprised. "What happened this time?"

I thought it sad that she had to add *this time*.

"It was the Christmas Festival, and we allowed people to use our restrooms. One of them stayed occupied far too long. I knocked, there was no answer, so I opened it with the key and found her on the floor."

Nana put her hand to her chest. "Oh, you poor sweet thing," she said.

"It's not the first time," I mumbled. "As you well know."

She patted my hand. "No, no, it's not, is it? You seem to have a penchant for these things."

I shook my head and swallowed. "No, that would mean I like it. And that's not the case. It just seems to happen to me."

"That it does," she said, shaking her head slowly. "Who?"

"Who?" I felt my eyebrows squish together.

"Who was it?" she said.

"Oh. One of Claire's clients."

"An older person, I assume? What happened?" she asked.

"No, she's quite young. Younger than me. And we don't know yet."

Nana's eyebrows shot up. "Did that man of yours show up?" She waved her hand. "Silly question. Of course, he showed up. For you."

Nana loves Levi and has relentlessly pushed for me to marry him. And she's not subtle about it. She's told me several times that men like that don't stay single long and won't wait around forever. I wasn't asking him to wait forever. I just wasn't ready *yet*.

"He did."

"And?" she pushed. She wasn't going to let this go.

"And what?"

"Melanie Hogan, stop being difficult," she scolded lightly.

I sighed. "He doesn't know, Nana." I drizzled honey on a slice of cornbread and stuffed a piece in my mouth. She waited for me to finish. "It's impossible to know without an autopsy."

"Surely he has a suspicion about the cause of death. Whether he thinks it's natural or not. Please tell me it was a natural death." She folded her hands together as if praying.

"They don't know. And that's the truth. I promise. I would tell you if I knew something."

She stood, took a glass mason jar from the cupboard, filled it with water, and set it gently in front of me.

"You don't have to wait on me, Nana. I should be the one waiting on you."

"Nonsense, dear. We're going to have so much fun tomorrow." She grinned and clapped her hands together in anticipation. Like mine, her mood lifted at the mention of our annual baking day. Her shoulders even appeared less weighted.

I smiled at her. "We are. I think I'm even starting to be more of a help than a hindrance."

"You're never a hindrance, child. But cleanup is less as the years go by."

I howled with laughter, nearly spitting out the drink of water I'd just taken. "That's a nice way of putting it."

My cell phone rang, and I plucked it from my coat pocket.

"Hey, Claire," I said.

"Melanie," she said, her voice telling me she was about to relay something that I didn't want to hear.

"What is it?" I asked, holding my breath.

"I've officially become a person of interest in the death of Patti Parker."

7

As soon as I got in the car to head home from Nana's, I hit Levi's number and put it on speaker. He answered on the second ring.

"I was starting to get worried," he said. "Where have you been?"

"Why didn't you tell me?" I asked.

"I called—"

"Levi, you should have told me." My voice sounded accusatory to my own ears; I could only imagine how it came across to him. But all I could think about was Claire right now. "You should have trusted me and told me about Claire."

"Melanie—"

"I just can't believe you—"

"Melanie," he said again, this time louder.

"What?"

"I called you. It went to voicemail. I left you a message."

My cheeks warmed. "You did?" I pulled the phone away from my ear and glanced at the little icon on the bottom of the screen. Sure enough, a missed call and a voicemail.

"Can we start this call over? Please?" I pleaded, feeling like an idiot. "Where Claire is concerned, I'm just a tad protective."

"Really?" he said, his voice gentle. "I never knew that."

"I'm sorry. I don't know why I didn't hear your call."

"It was a while ago, so—"

"Tell me you don't believe Claire could be a suspect."

"It doesn't matter what I think. Cole is off the case. And they'll probably take it from me and give it to Walker."

"Because of me?"

"Because of all of us. I'm too close to it."

"Claire needs you to stay on it. Is there any way they will let you?"

"I'm ninety-nine percent sure that won't happen." My mind started spinning with ideas. As if he could hear my thoughts through the phone, he said, "No," firmly.

"No what?" I asked.

"You know what," he said. I could almost see him run his hand over his bald head out of frustration. "I know you, Melanie. Promise me you won't get involved in this," he pleaded.

I hesitated for a moment. "I promise I'll be very, very careful. How's that?"

I heard an exhale escape through pursed lips. I was getting to know that sound all too well. I peered in my rearview mirror and switched lanes as soon as it was safe to exit onto my road.

"If this were your best friend, you wouldn't just sit back and let the process happen, Levi. Admit it."

"There's a difference," he countered. "I'm a cop, and you're not."

"I have my concealed carry permit," I reminded him. He stayed quiet, contemplating how to handle this best, no doubt. How to best handle me so I wouldn't get involved.

As if reading my mind, he said, "You absolutely cannot get involved in the police investigation. It makes it harder on the detective handling the case. You will compromise Walker's work."

"I don't intend to get involved in the police investigation," I said.

He sighed and muttered, "Thank God."

"I plan on doing my own investigation."

He groaned. "You're going to kill me one of these days. You know that, right?"

"You knew what you were getting into when we started dating. It's not too late to change your mind."

"Yeah? Is that what you want?" he asked.

I heard the sting in his tone. "No," I said quickly. "That is not what I want. But I am who I am. My friends are important to me, and I will stop at nothing to help them.

"I admire your loyalty to your friends and family. I just worry."

"That's not such a bad thing, is it?" I smiled to myself. "I worry about you, too, but I've never asked you to change." He didn't say anything, so I continued. "So what's the deal? With Patti's death. What made them decide it's murder?"

"I don't have details. As far as I know, they aren't a hundred percent and haven't filed it with the District Attorney yet."

I took a deep breath, letting the calm work its way through me. In the past, once Levi adjusted to the fact that I wouldn't wait for his blessing before doing something, he accepted it and worked with me as much as possible without compromising the investigation. He probably thought it was better to be part of my nosing around so that he could keep abreast of what I found than to be in the dark and caught off-guard.

"So there's still a chance it wasn't murder." It was a statement more to myself, out of relief, than to Levi. I chewed on my lower lip.

"There are too many indicators that it wasn't a natural death, Mel. I think we're looking at murder. Of course, I don't have all the details. They're keeping me on the outskirts."

"Like the rash on her cheeks, petechia —"

"How did you find out about all of that?"

"Babe, my office is right across the hall from the restroom where you guys discussed all of that."

"But we were almost whispering. I could hardly hear what was said, and I was right there."

"Guess my hearing is better than yours."

He chuckled. "You're impossible. But I love you anyway."

Warmth spread from my head to my toes. I never tired of hearing those words. Each time was like the first time.

"I love you, too." The line went silent, yet neither of us wanted to hang up.

I approached a house on the corner of my final turn off. It practically levitated with light energy as the red, green, and white lights reflected off the white snow that blanketed the acreage around the house. Numerous pine trees scattered about the yard blinked with alternating red, green, and white lights, as did the split rail fence that circled the property.

"I've been so wrapped up in our conversation I haven't even noticed the lights until now," I said. "That's my favorite part of the drive during Christmastime."

"They were probably multicolored anyway," he teased.

Levi and I agreed to disagree on our choice of Christmas lights. He was a multicolored light fan all the way. I loved white lights. The ones around my deck I kept up all year long. There was something about a log house and white lights that satisfied me immensely. Nana, on the other hand, liked her multicolored lights like Levi, and as much as I was at Nana's house, I got the best of both worlds.

After a few more exchanges, we hung up, and I turned into my driveway. My outdoor Christmas lights were on a timer and sparkled brightly against the pristine snow. I parked in my detached garage, wondering, once again, why I kept procrastinating on adding a garage onto my house. Change and I weren't best friends, but in this case, I would welcome it. That being said, during the summer, I enjoyed the short hike between the garage and the house, the smell of damp earth in the evenings and early mornings from the dew, the burst of fresh air appealing to my senses. But wintertime in Minnesota…well, that was a different story. *Someday*, I promised myself.

I carefully plodded to the house around snow that had drifted along the sides of the narrow path. Snowfall hasn't been atrocious this year as it has been in previous years, but the cold has been brutal. With each breath I exhaled, it looked like I was doing some serious vaping. It appeared to crystalize in the air until the next breath.

I reached the house none too soon. My cheeks were numb, and I was pretty sure I could no longer move my lips to form a coherent word. I should have stayed overnight at Nana's since I was going back in the morning, but the minute I opened my front door, that thought vanished. The scent of vanilla from a scent diffuser and pine from my Christmas tree greeted my nostrils, and the problems of the day melted to nothing. Away from the hustle and bustle of town, living out here in the country was sheer bliss. The only sounds were that of the birds in the mornings, chittering squirrels, occasional snowmobiles rumbling across the lake in the winter, and the low rhythmic hum of the fishing boats trolling along the water in the summer.

Claire had even come to love it, the city girl that she used to be. Little more than a year ago, she moved out here, just across the field and grove of trees from my house. We could look out our windows, see the other's outside light, and often use it as a signal to let the other know we were home and safe. Tonight, I observed her red and white Christmas lights shining on her back porch. My heart felt heavy for her.

I set my purse and bag on the kitchen chair next to the door, slipped out of my boots and coat, and kept my eyes on Claire's lights across the field. I had to think of a way to clear her. But maybe, just maybe, despite the speculation thus far, the autopsy would do that, proving it wasn't a murder at all. I doubted it, but it didn't hurt to hold onto hope.

I pinched together the tiers of my sunshine yellow curtains in the kitchen window, went into the living room, and plopped down on the sofa, clutching a caramel-colored throw pillow to my chest. I leaned back, rested my head against the cushion, and stared at the string of white lights around the large picture window that overlooked the lake.

I replayed the events of the day, wondering how we'd gotten here. Again. Wasn't one death in the salon enough? What were the odds that there would be two? And both murder? But I did know one thing:

if foul play was determined, I would move hell and high water to clear Claire's name. I'm sure Detective Walker was okay, but he wasn't Levi. And he didn't have the motivation that Levi and I had.

I slapped the pillow I'd been clutching down on the couch, stood, and headed for the stairs to my bedroom in the loft. I told Nana I would be there by seven, and I needed to get some shut-eye if I was going to function tomorrow and help her rather than hinder. I'd reached the top of the stairs when my phone rang. I glanced at the display.

"Hey, Claire."

"You alone?" Her voice was missing the usual joviality.

"If you're asking if Levi is here, no, he's not. Why?"

"Can I come by for a minute?"

"Of course. But what about Syd? Isn't she in bed by now?"

"Cole said he'd sit with her for a while."

"Come on over. Door'll be open."

8

Before Claire arrived, I changed into a pair of black sweatpants and a green University of Minnesota hoodie Jack gave me years ago. Jack is the third party of mine and Claire's trio turned quartet when Rubie came along. He lives in Minneapolis but comes to see us frequently; so frequently, in fact, that the spare room in my house has turned into a guest room for him. He's a clothing and jewelry designer and sells his product, Jack's Originals, in salons all over the state, including ours.

I picked up my phone and punched in a text to him.

Hey, stranger. Haven't talked for over a week. Lots to catch you up on. Coming up this weekend?

I watched the three little dots dancing under my text, letting me know he was reading and typing something back.

Can't this weekend. With my mom. My dad's here in the hospital. Heart attack. Will talk later.

My heart fell. Poor Jack. I texted back, *Keep me posted. Sending my love.*

A second later, *XOXO* popped up on my screen.

I tossed my phone on my bed, swept my hair back into a messy ponytail, and washed off the little makeup I had on. I wasn't a typical hairstylist. My hair was a simple, highlighted layered cut and hung a few inches below my shoulders, and I wore little makeup. As in just mascara and lip gloss. Sometimes I played it dangerous and threw on some blush, but not often. Claire always told me she envied my flawless creamy skin. I envied hers. Never happy with what we have, I supposed. Which is why people come into the salon all day long, every day, to get something other than what they had. *An ungrateful bunch we humans are*, I thought.

Claire knocked once and opened the door. I jogged over in my stocking feet and greeted her with a hug.

"Hey there, my friend. How are you?"

"Better now."

I held my hand out for her coat. "Come on," I said, laying it over a chair and leading her into the living room.

"I can't stay long. My little monster might wake up and give Cole a hard time."

The love in her voice for Sydney, her *little monster*, was apparent. I grinned. "How's my bug? Does she know anything?"

"She's doing okay. And, no, I don't want her knowing anything at this point."

"How are she and Cole getting along?"

She hinted at a smile. "Cole is really trying with her, but she's making him earn every bit of her trust."

Claire had waited a long time before she allowed the two of them to meet. Sydney's dad, Tyler, was killed overseas while on duty when she was four. Claire's dating life had been nearly non-existent, not that she hadn't had numerous offers. Over the years, it seemed like she'd received the entire stock of a floral shop at the salon, bouquet by bouquet. But she was never interested. The day Cole snagged her, taking her off the market, there were broken hearts across the town.

"She'll come around," I said. "She's just staking her territory."

"She's relentless," Claire said with a sigh. "But, Mel, he is so good with her." She met my eyes and smiled, revealing the endearing gap between her front teeth. "He gives her all the space she needs and is so careful not to take my time away from her. I don't know how I got so lucky."

I grinned and hugged her. "He's the one who got lucky, Claire. Can I get you something to drink?"

"No. I just needed to come over for a minute. You know, draw on your strength. Cole is so upset over this whole thing and so worried about me. I almost feel like I need to hide it from him, that I'm worried at all. What did your grandmother say?"

I scrunched up my face. "I didn't tell her that part."

Claire's eyes grew big. "Weren't you there when I called?"

"Yeah. But I didn't want to worry her before bed. I'll fill her in on that part tomorrow, but only if I have to. She doesn't have to know everything." Then I had an idea. "Hey! Do you and Syd want to come with me tomorrow to her house for our annual Christmas baking day?"

"Can I let you know in the morning?"

"Tell you what," I said, "you two sleep in, do your mother-daughter stuff in the morning and come to my grandmother's house whenever you're ready. We'll do the sugar cookie cut-outs first, and Sydney can help frost them."

Claire beamed, the light returning to her eyes. "Oh! She would love that! And so would I!"

"It's a deal."

She got up and slipped into her coat and boots. "See you tomorrow afternoon sometime."

"Hey, Claire?" I asked as she readied to open the door.

"Yeah?"

"Depending on what they find in the autopsy, let's meet here tomorrow night. You, me, and Rubie." And then, "Let's just meet regardless. It's been a while."

"Shall I call Jack?"

I shook my head. "His dad is in the hospital in Minneapolis. Heart attack."

Claire gasped. "When?"

"Found out just before you got here." My heart felt heavier if that was even possible.

"Why didn't you tell me before now?"

It wasn't an accusation but rather a simple question. One that brought to mind those exact words I'd spoken to Levi earlier this evening.

"You had enough on your plate when you got here. I didn't want to worry you." Guilt invaded my headspace. Had Levi told me that, I would have been furious. "I'm sorry. I should have told you right away."

"It's okay. You meant well," she said with a sigh, then leaned over to hug me.

The guilt was now even stronger. I should have been this forgiving with Levi. And he hadn't even withheld anything from me.

"I'm not sure if his dad is seeing Jack or not, but I'm sure he wants to be there for his mom."

Jack's dad wrote him off when Jack came out and told him he was gay. His dad had forbidden Jack's mother to have him over to the house, so they met in a restaurant whenever Jack saw her. Jack pretended it didn't bother him, but I knew it did. And that's why he understood my issues with Violet so well.

"Jack's dad will regret it someday," Claire said, shaking her head slowly. "I just hope it's not too late."

"See you tomorrow there, sunshine," I said, closing the door behind her.

***

Sleep mostly escaped me that night. I had dreams of Claire behind bars in a bright orange jumpsuit with matching hair scarf and dreams of Jack trying to get into his dad's hospital room, fighting past security guards holding him back. I dreamt of Patti standing and walking out of the restroom after the coroner pronounced her dead. I even had one where I was in jail, and Rubie brought me her pink boots. I awoke tangled in my blankets and with my pillow on the floor.

I stretched and got up, feeling as though I'd run a marathon. This day could be an interesting one. Sometimes I was dangerous in the kitchen after I've had enough sleep, much less with none.

I began my usual routine of coffee, devotional, and reading the paper from my tablet, but coffee was about all I could focus on. The rest was but a blur. I finally resigned myself to the fact that my routine would not happen and jumped in the shower. Forty-five minutes later, dressed in ratty jeans and a black tank under a black sweatshirt, I headed for Nana's.

I looked down Claire's driveway as I drove by. All was quiet. Not sure what I expected at this hour. I contemplated calling Levi but decided to wait until a bit later in case he got called out last night.

White gauzy haze hung in the air, and the bare tree branches were white bony arms reaching for the sky. Despite having to dress in multiple layers until one could hardly move, I always loved this part of winter. Summer was my favorite, but since winter was a given, I might as well find something to enjoy about it. I smiled and took a sip of coffee from my travel mug. I drove in silence without the radio for the duration of the drive, solely focusing on the pure beauty around me.

Nana already had her Christmas lights on. I'd wondered if she even turned them off last night. Since she had an artificial tree with LED lights, I wasn't too concerned with anything other than her electric bill. Because she really loved her lights. I couldn't break myself from the need for the scent of pine and had to have a real tree every year.

I pulled up in front of her garage and let myself in through the door in the breezeway. The rattling of pans and the tinkling of glass bowls greeted me.

"Nana?" I called. "I'm here." I winced when I heard a loud crash, then clattering, clanging, and a bang. I slipped my boots off on the rug.

She came around the corner, beaming and adorned in her Mrs. Claus Christmas apron. "Come, come, dear!" She handed me a red and white checked apron.

I held it up, inspecting it. "You still don't have a black one?" I teased.

She laughed. "Oh, you!"

I took off my coat and slipped the apron over my head. "Everything okay in the kitchen? Sounded like something broke."

"No, nothing that dramatic. Just wrestling some pans from the cabinet is all. Dropped one or two." After getting a good glimpse of me, her smile faded.

"Don't take this wrong, dontcha know, but you look like you've been up all night."

I tilted my head to the side, then nodded. "More or less."

She frowned. "Did you hear something about the gal that died in your salon?"

I took a deep breath. Might as well get it over with. She'd know if I was holding something back anyway. I was surprised she didn't pick up on it last evening after Claire called me. But I'd only stayed a couple of minutes and excused myself to go home. I twisted a strand of hair around my finger and took a deep breath.

"Ok, Nana, it sounds really bad," I said, trying to ease into it as best I could. I took another deep breath. "Claire is a suspect in Patti's death."

Nana gasped. "What—"

I rushed on. "Patti was in a catfight with another woman in line for a free haircut. She—Patti, not Claire—got hot cocoa dumped on her during the fight. Claire went out, broke it up, got Patti a cup of hot coffee, and then led Patti to the restroom to clean up. Sometime in the next hour, Patti died." I held my hand up and crossed my fingers. "They still haven't officially ruled it a homicide, so I'm holding out hope."

Nana was clearly upset. Her brows furrowed, and the sparkle in her eyes changed from joy to sparks of anger. "Well, surely they know that sweet child wouldn't hurt a fly." She suddenly calmed a bit, and she nodded. "That man of yours will clear her." I stayed silent and averted my gaze. "Won't he?" she persisted.

"Well..."

"Melanie?" she demanded. "He will clear her, right?"

"Nana, Levi can't be on the case because of me, my relationship with Claire, and—well, you can understand the problem with that. I'm going to see what I can find out."

She watched me for what seemed like hours. Funny how that look could still make me squirm.

Finally, she said, "Okay."

"Wh—what?" I stammered. Surely I'd misheard.

"I said okay. But I'm going to be having a chat with Levi, dontcha know."

"I'm sure you are." A person would be hard-pressed to find someone kinder and more giving than my grandmother, but there's also no one in the world more protective when it comes to the people she loves. "I invited Claire and Sydney to join us later today. I hope that's okay."

"You betcha it's okay," she said.

"I thought it might be fun to have Sydney here to frost the sugar cookie cut-outs."

"Perfect." Light came back to her eyes.

She loved Sydney as if she were her own granddaughter. And as spoiled as Sydney was, by me more than anyone else, she was always on her best behavior around my grandmother.

I picked up a pan that still lay on the floor from when I'd arrived. I pulled my hair back in a ponytail, pushed up my sleeves, washed my hands, and began rolling some of her pre-made dough from the refrigerator.

The morning flew by as we stirred, poured, rolled, sprinkled, baked, joked, sang to Christmas carols, and tested the goods. The pastries from the bakery remained forgotten in the bag. By one o'clock, when I thought I might crash from a sugar rush, my phone rang. I grabbed it with fingers dusted with powdered sugar. Levi! Darn! I'd forgotten to call him after the uncomfortable conversation with my grandmother when I'd first arrived.

"Hi, handsome," I said, licking powdered sugar from my fingertips.

"Are you sitting down?"

I turned away from my grandmother as I felt the color drain from my face, and my legs turned weak at his somber tone. And here I was having such a good day. I hadn't even felt tired from too little sleep.

"I'm not going to like what you're about to say, am I?"

"Nope."

I twisted a strand of hair around my finger. "Murder?"

"Yup. They're filing the case first thing in the morning."

9

The line fell silent as I felt my grandmother's attention on me.

"You there?" Levi asked.

I cleared my throat. "Uh, yeah. What does this mean for Claire?"

"I think we both know the answer to that question."

"When this whole thing is over, you and I deserve a weekend off somewhere, away from anything resembling murder. Just you and me." Levi was silent. "Hello? No?"

"Yes!" he said. "It's just that this is the first time you've suggested some time away."

After the words had come out of my mouth, I was as surprised as he was.

"We've earned it," I said quietly.

"Yes, we have," he murmured.

"Well, this means I have fast work to do," I said and exhaled the breath I'd been holding. "Does Claire know yet?"

"Not unless Cole defied orders and told her."

"So that could be a yes or a no." Cole was the biggest rule-follower I'd ever known, but he was also head over heels for Claire and would do anything to protect her. As if on cue, the doorbell rang. "She's here," I said.

"Claire?"

"Yeah. She and Sydney are joining Nana and me for cookie frosting."

He chuckled. "I would hate to see that kitchen by the time you're done."

"You mean by the time Sydney's done," I corrected him.

"No. I meant what I said."

"You're very naughty, Levi Wescott."

After a response inappropriate for anyone else's ears, I hung up and went to meet Claire and Sydney.

Nana took my lead and didn't mention anything about Levi's call for the entire afternoon. Luck was on my side because Claire silenced her phone and tucked it inside her purse, claiming she didn't want any distractions. I followed suit and put mine away as well. Nana just winked at me and nodded her approval discreetly.

Bing Crosby's "White Christmas" played from Nana's stereo. She had every Christmas album of his, and I knew that we'd have listened to every one of them by the end of the day.

I dumped powdered sugar into several different bowls, adding enough milk for the perfect consistency and a splash of vanilla in each. Claire opened the numerous bottles of decorations and set them on the table. We had multi-colored dots, sprinkles of blue, red, green, and yellow, red hots, chocolate sprinkles, mini chocolate chips, and pieces of licorice strips, both red and black. Nana and Sydney collected butter knives for frosting, toothpicks for the finer details, and lots and lots of paper towels.

As Claire, Syd, and I sat down to begin our masterpieces, Nana poured each of us a cup of hot cinnamon cider with the ladle from the pot on the stove. It was all so perfect that I even managed to forget about the dark cloud Levi had delivered earlier. At least for a little while. Claire was carefree, laughing, loving up on Syd, and acted as though she didn't have anything going on other than what was right here right now. And then I remembered that sometime by the end of the day, I had to tell her what I'd found out. It was only right. I felt a rock in the pit of my stomach.

"Hey, Nana," I said, forcing my mind from the unpleasant task as long as I could. "Remember when Granddad helped us do this one year?"

She laughed at the memory. "Oh, yes. One year and he was fired."

Syd's eyes grew large. "Who fired him?" she asked.

"She did," I said, laughing and pointing at my grandmother. "Granddad was worse in the kitchen than I was."

"Not possible!" Syd razzed.

"Watch it there, little missy." I narrowed my eyes at her and spread some green frosting on the tip of her nose.

She giggled, and it was music to my ears.

By the time we finished, we had frosted cutouts everywhere there had been space. There were angels, snowmen, Christmas trees, gingerbread boys—and girls—stars, elves, and Santas.

When Sydney got up to go find my grandmother's cat, Claire whispered to me, "Did you ever find out who was masquerading as Santa and the elf yesterday at the festival?"

I shook my head. "No. But now that..." I trailed off. I hadn't intended to say anything yet. Not like this.

"Now that what?" she asked, eyes wide with interest.

Her innocence made this even harder. "Nothing."

"Melanie," my grandmother said. I looked at her, and her gaze held mine, her blue eyes a little darker.

I glanced around to make sure Sydney wasn't within earshot and took a deep breath before saying, "Patti's death was a homicide. They're filing the case with the District Attorney in the morning."

Claire's brows furrowed. "I already know that."

I gasped. "You *knew*? Why didn't you say anything?"

Nana stood and began puttering by the sink, giving us some privacy.

"Because I didn't think you knew, and I didn't want to spoil the afternoon. I wanted to have a fun time, just the four of us, before hell ensues." She exhaled, propped her elbow on the table, and rested her head on the back of her hand. She took a slow, calming breath and sat back in her chair.

"But—but—" I studied her a moment. "How are you so calm if you knew?"

"I'm a mother. I have lots of practice holding it together." She half-smiled at her attempt to lighten the dark mood that had settled in. I sat back and noticed the music had stopped, making everything quieter yet.

I abruptly stood and began cleaning up the table. "Nana, you must be exhausted after all of this." Frosted shapes, nutmeg logs, spritzes, teatime tassies, gingerbread, peanut butter blossoms, pecan snowballs, and jam thumbprints covered every inch of the countertops, butcher block island, and table. "Why don't you go rest. I'll do the cleanup."

"I'll help," Claire said. "And so will Sydney."

"I want to stay in the living room with Grandma Rose," Sydney said.

"You helped make the mess, you can help clean the mess," Claire said.

"Nana would enjoy her company," I said.

"Thanks, Aunt Mel," Sydney said, beaming.

Claire scolded me without saying a word. Finally, she said, "And people wonder why she's spoiled."

"I'm not spoiled, mama, I'm loovvved," she purred, smiling and revealing teeth still too big for her mouth. Her dark hair was getting so long she'd be able to sit on it pretty soon.

"Girl, you need a haircut," I said, pulling it back into a ponytail.

"I wanna see how long I can get it," she said.

"You know what they say about the hair stylist's kid," I joked.

"Yeah, yeah." Claire laughed and waved her hand in dismissal. "And the doctor's kid, the shrink's kid, yada yada yada." With one last hug around Claire's waist, Syd followed Nana into the living room. "And just like that, she escapes from work again."

With Claire and I left alone in the kitchen, we had some time to talk some more.

"Now that we know Patti's death was murder—" I stopped and turned to look at her. "How are you doing about that, by the way. Not the person of interest piece of it, but you knew her."

Claire shrugged. "I'm not sure."

My jaw dropped. "What?" She was tough as nails about her own issues but as soft as an overripe banana when she saw someone, whether human or animal, hurting.

She lifted her hands by her sides, palms up, then shrugged. "It's not like we were close."

I took a step backward and studied her. "I know. But she was still your client." Maybe the person of interest thing was hitting her harder than I'd even thought.

She clenched her teeth together, appeared as if she was struggling with saying something, then said, "I hope I'm not struck by lightning for saying this, but Patti was not a nice person." Then she whispered, "In fact, she was *mean.*" She flinched as though she expected God to strike her down.

She picked up two bowls from the table and scraped the remaining frosting into a Tupperware container I'd pulled from the cabinet. As a kid, I'd always loved the leftover frosting on graham crackers and still do to this day.

I tossed a dishtowel over my shoulder, grabbed two bowls, and followed suit. "So there won't be a lack of suspects."

"Sadly, no," she agreed.

We worked in tandem for a while, neither of us speaking. I ran through possibilities in my head and assumed Claire was doing the same thing. Which was unusual for her, however. She was the extrovert of us two, and her thoughts usually tumbled out of her mouth as she thought them through.

When the dishwasher was loaded and started, and the towels hung to dry, I covered the cookies securely. Nana would package them tomorrow to give as gifts for friends and neighbors from both of us. As per our annual routine, we would also bring a good-sized platter to the homeless shelter. I turned out the lights save for the one above the kitchen sink, and we each took a seat at the kitchen table. Flour, frosting, and God only knows what else clung to my hoodie. I pushed the sleeves up and studied Claire through the warm amber glow of the dim kitchen lighting and the Christmas lights. She stood up, peeked into the living room, and sat back down.

"Syd's snuggled right up against Grandma Rose, and they're reading a book," Claire said gently, her eyes misting. "What if—"

"No!" I said, shaking my head. "Just no. Don't finish that sentence. We are going to clear your name, Claire."

"How?"

"Are you kidding me?" I said, my hand coming down on the table harder than I'd intended. I waited for a moment to be sure Sydney didn't come into the room. "I can't believe you just asked me that."

"But—"

"Claire," I said as if she was Syd's age. "First of all, you're not guilty of anything. Second of all, have I not proven myself in the past?"

"Yeah, but—"

"But nothin', my friend."

"Are you going to let me finish a sentence?"

"Sure. If it's a sentence I want to hear." I grinned.

She chuckled softly. "You're impossible."

"I am going to find out who killed Patti, Claire. I promise you."

She nodded, her eyes wide, and crossed her arms in front of her as if protecting herself. "That kind of scares me if you want the truth. You doing whatever it is you're going to do to find out and all."

"Trust me," I said with a wink that she met with an eye roll. "Let the girl ride home with me. We need some alone time, she and I." I watched Claire, hopeful, and she leaned over and hugged me. Nonverbal answers were my favorite.

10

Sydney talked a mile a minute on the ride home. That cute little lisp of hers—getting less and less noticeable as she got older—kept me entertained as she told me about a boy in school who keeps pulling the strings on her hoodies, a teacher who wears her skirts too short, and about one of her friends who started wearing a bra when she doesn't even need one. Of all those she told me, this story was by far the biggest disgrace in her eyes.

"Aunt Mel," she'd said, "she wears shirts that show other kids she wears a bra. She looks like a hussy!"

I cracked up, which earned me a dirty look and a scolding that put Nana's scoldings to shame. "Where in the world did you ever hear that word, young lady?"

"TV," she said, proudly jutting her chin.

"Well, I'd say you should maybe watch some different TV shows, kiddo. Better yet, read a book. And none that contain the word 'hussy' or anything of the like." I laughed again, which this time earned me a slap on the arm.

We followed Claire into the driveway. I pulled my car close to the house and waited for them to get inside. When the door closed behind them, I made a mad dash to my little log haven. I had a date with my whiteboard until Levi got there. I glanced at my watch as I jogged to the door through the icy cold air. Seven on the dot. I had to move it if I would get something workable in place before he got there. I wanted at least a skeleton of something on that board.

The Christmas lights had all come on at six except for the tree lights. Those weren't on a timer. I'd heard about too many fires caused by lights on a too-dry tree. Even though I made sure my tree stayed watered, it was a chance I wasn't willing to take.

The tree now fully lit, the dancing lights making it feel alive, I took the stairs two at a time to my loft bedroom, glancing toward the lake from the windows that lined the wall along the stairs. Lights from several snowmobiles bobbed over snowdrifts on the lake. I shivered at the thought of how cold they must be.

I changed from my baking clothes into a pair of yoga pants and a sweatshirt, washed my face, and ran a brush through my hair. Next, I snagged the whiteboard from my closet, dry erase markers in red, green, and black, and headed back downstairs to start a fire in the fireplace.

Done with the prepping, I glanced at my smartwatch. I had about forty-five minutes. Unless he was early.

I wrote Patti's name in the center of the board and started making what resembled spokes from the circle around her name. At the end of each one, I wrote a potential person of interest. So far, I had Santa, Elf, Trudy, Jenny, and Claire. I had to include Claire so I could rule her out by lack of evidence. I extended extra spokes from the circle with Patti's name in case I come across more 'people of interest.' By the time I finished, each name had acquired two more, one with the word *Motive* and the other with the word *Opportunity*.

I stepped back to look at the whole when headlights reflected off the large picture window on the wall that faced the lake, directly across the house from the front kitchen window. I glanced at the clock. He was early.

Levi opened the door just before I reached it. I lifted on my tiptoes, swiped the Birch Haven Police Department wool hat from his bald head, and kissed his frozen lips.

"Welcome, Detective," I purred.

113

"Well, hello there," he said as he circled an arm around my waist, pulling me closer to him. He playfully rubbed his stubble beard against my neck, and I squealed like a little girl and pushed away from him.

I waggled my finger at him. "No more kisses for you, mister!" He made a move to chase me, but I yelled, "Boots! Boots! Take your boots off before you take another step, buddy!"

He scoffed and slipped off one SOREL boot, then the other, and set them by the door. "You have such strict rules in this house."

"My house," I corrected him. "I have strict rules at my house."

"As you've reminded me several times. One day, though, this will be ours. Unless you want to move into mine."

My jaw dropped. "I am not moving from this house."

He raised his eyebrows and pulled me toward him again. "You seem pretty set on that. What if—" He saw over my shoulder and into the living room and chuckled. "You started your investigation already?"

"You're surprised? I thought you knew me better than that."

"But you couldn't have been home from your grandmother's for more than a half-hour." He skirted around me and into the living room, stood in front of the board.

"Not much more than that," I agreed, planting myself beside him.

"You just can't *not* get involved, can you?" he asked, looking at me and then back at the board.

"Not when the life of my best friend hangs in the balance because of it."

"Or when you're just simply curious," he countered.

"Not true." My chin tilted up ever so slightly. "If that were the case, I would be in your hair all the time."

"You're naturally defiant, aren't you? Besides, I don't have hair."

"Some people would agree with that statement, yes. The defiant statement. Everyone would agree with the no-hair one." I snickered but got serious again quickly. "But," I held up a finger, "if you ever needed my help, you could rest assured I would move heaven and earth to be there for you."

"I do know that," he said. "But since you've promised time away with me after this is over, I'm willing to be in on this little side investigation you've got going since I can't be in on the police one. Let's get this thing wrapped up." He winked at me and smiled. His phone rang, he glanced at the number and groaned. "You've got to be kidding me," he grumbled. He paused a moment before tapping the screen. "Wescott."

I watched as he listened intently to the person on the other end. After several times of muttering "okay," "uh-huh," "yeah," he hung up. He looked at me, his gray-green eyes looking tired. "I hate to do this—in fact, you have no idea how much I hate it— but I have to go."

"Work?" I stuck out my lip.

"A body down by the river. Looks like a transient. This cold snap is deadly for them." He started back toward the kitchen.

"I wish they would all go to the shelter," I said.

"There's not enough room in the shelter for everyone," he said. "We need another one in town. Either that or a much larger one."

"What's sad is there are so many people who are homeless."

He met my eyes, grinned, and held his hand out to me. "Why don't you use your investigative talents to find a way to fix that instead of solving murders."

"Detective Westcott, are you afraid I'm taking over your job?" I ribbed him. I allowed him to pull me toward him. "Besides, if this were your case, I wouldn't have to be investigating it now, would I? You have your department to thank for that."

"The department is going by the book. We have rules and policies. My being on this case would be a clear violation." He shrugged a shoulder. "But it's not a violation to be in on yours."

"Does this mean you're working for me now?" I grinned.

His look said more than any words could have and I laughed. "See ya later, Second in Command."

As soon as Levi left, I locked up and sat in front of the fire while staring at the whiteboard. My information was too limited at this point to fill in any more details. But tomorrow...well, tomorrow I would make a point of uncovering as much as I could. And I had all morning before doing our free haircut extravaganza in the afternoon. And after that, Claire and Rubie were coming to my house to go over theories and brainstorm. But before we did, I had to get as much information as I could.

I stood and stretched, put the fire out, and headed upstairs. It was going to be a long and busy day tomorrow.

11

My phone woke me the next morning. I cracked open an eye and glanced at my bedside clock. Six-o-seven. Groggy from sleep that eluded me again, I reached for my nightstand and fumbled for my phone but dropped it on the floor. I groaned and reached down to grasp it.

"Hello?" I said without looking at caller ID first.

"Good morning, Blondie."

I smiled at the sound of Levi's voice and pushed my bed-head hair out of my face. "Hey."

"I'm not used to you sleeping past five-thirty. Everything okay?"

"Yeah, good." I lay back down and pulled the covers up to my chin. "How was your case last night?"

"Unless we find out differently, it's just as we thought."

"Hm. Sad." I thought about the family this person had out there somewhere. How their world would be turned upside down for Christmas. It made me think of Patti. "Has anyone been in contact with Patti's family?"

"Our policy is for an officer and a victim advocate to notify them in person. I'm sure they did it by now."

"Sad," I mumbled again. What a way to wake up.

"Did you do any more brainstorming last night?"

"No. I don't have enough information yet. I'm heading in early today before free haircuts this afternoon to see if I can find out anything." I stood, taking one of the blankets with me, and wrapped it around my shoulders. "You'll let me know if you hear anything, won't you?" Silence met my question. "Won't you?" I repeated.

"Yes."

"Promise?" I asked.

"I promise I will tell you what I can."

"Meh." Better than nothing, I supposed.

"They're not going to let me in on the information if I'm banned from the case. But I did find out the name of the elf."

My eyes popped open, and I clutched the blanket tighter. "Are you kidding me? You're just going to spring that on me like that? When did you find out?"

"Last night."

"Walker told you?"

"No."

"Who?"

"Someone else."

As vague as he was, that wasn't my concern right now. "What I meant is who was the elf?"

"Name is Della Birk."

I squinted with recognition yet couldn't remember where I'd heard the name. "Della Birk," I repeated. "Where have I heard that before?"

"I'm sure you'll figure it out," Levi said. "I know you will."

I chuckled. "Love the confidence you have in me."

"I'd say it's more that I know your determination. Not to mention the practice you've had of late."

I cocked my head to the side as I pondered this. "Yeah, that works." I glanced at the clock. "Hey, thanks for waking me up. I gotta get going."

I headed for the shower and finished up with ten minutes of standing under steaming hot water until it started getting cold. I'd considered getting a bigger water heater a time or two, but this one was fine for now.

Eventually, I got out and toweled off at record speed before wrapping my robe around me again. Turning down my heat at night had a double benefit—I slept better when it was colder, and it got my blood moving in the morning when I crawled out from beneath my covers.

I dried my hair, let the natural waves hang loose, and slipped into a black and white turtleneck sweater, black jeans, and black high heeled boots. After reading a devotional while eating toast and coffee, I washed my dishes and laid them out in the dish drainer. Before I scooted out the door, I turned back to the living room and studied the whiteboard. I erased *Elf* with the palm of my hand and inserted *Della Birk*. One step closer, a hundred more to go. It would have been intimidating had I not been so psyched to get at least one piece of information.

Turning to leave again, I went back a second time to skim through the newspaper on my tablet. It was usually my routine to check every morning what happened in Birch Haven the day before. The fact that I hadn't followed routine this morning was proof positive I was more worried about Claire than I'd thought. Routine and I were best friends.

I slipped back out of my coat and hung it on a chair, then snagged my tablet, touched the power button, and perched on a stool at the kitchen island as I waited for it to come to life. How could I have not checked the paper for news about Patti? Surely they'd gotten wind of it by now that it wasn't a natural death. I hoped Claire's name wasn't attached to that news story if it was there. Since Levi lacked information about why they ruled it a homicide, I hoped the media could enlighten me.

As soon as the tablet pulled up the paper, my breath caught. Frontpage, center stage, was the headline, *Body Found at Hair Salon Ruled as a Homicide.* I closed my eyes, willing the story to disappear. I opened one eye. Nope, still there. *Great!* This was one morning I hoped Sydney would be needy, so Claire didn't have time to look at the paper. She didn't need to be reminded of it first thing.

I went on to read it more thoroughly.

Local police have ruled the death of Birch Haven resident, Patti Parker, as a homicide. Ms. Parker was found on the floor of a restroom at A Cut Above Hair Salon owned by Melanie Hogan and Claire Davis. The salon was giving out free haircuts as part of the Annual Christmas Festival. Additional details to follow as the investigation unfolds. Neither Ms. Hogan nor Ms. Davis could be reached for comment.

I reached for my phone and looked at the screen for any missed calls. "You never called, bozos," I muttered. I read through it again, disappointed I didn't know anything more now than I did before. I'd learned in the past how sneaky the media could be to garner information. Unfortunately, this wasn't one of those times. I refreshed the screen in hopes that there would be an addition to what I'd read. No such luck.

Thank God they didn't have a list of suspects. Or 'persons of interest,' as the police referred to Claire. They were the same in my book. Perhaps they believed 'person of interest' sounded less frightening, but anyone with half a brain knew it was the same thing. I've told Levi that in the past, to which he'd just smirked, knowing it was in his best interest not to confuse me with the facts when I had my mind made up.

I stayed perched on a stool at the kitchen island and absently tapped my finger on the countertop until the tablet timed out and went dark. I had to find out why they ruled it a homicide. What evidence did they uncover? Detective Walker and the rest of the police were most likely informed to keep all information from Cole and Levi for the integrity of the investigation. I could try to get a copy of the autopsy report. Someone once told me the preliminary report could be obtained in a couple of days. But that's in the case of a natural death. Certainly, homicides were different. And I heard toxicology reports could take as long as six to eight weeks. Levi found Oxy pills beside Patti's body, but they wouldn't know whether she overdosed on those or not yet. *Would they?* I could at least see if I could get a copy of the preliminary report and start there. If not, I would have to find a different starting place.

I slipped back into my coat, wrapped a scarf around my neck, grabbed my leather mittens, and out the door I went.

The icy air pinched my cheeks, and thick vapor materialized with each breath. I swear my nostrils even stuck together when I breathed. My eyes watered.

I had plugged in the block heater on my car last night in addition to parking in the garage, so it groaned to life with little resistance. Non-Minnesotans think we're crazy for plugging in our cars. Until they've spent one winter night here. Then they get it.

I let my car warm up for a few minutes before creeping up my driveway toward the road. I glanced toward Claire's house. The lights were still out. Hopefully, she was able to sleep in for a while.

As I neared town, the roads became busier with Monday morning business traffic. By the time I reached the salon, I would have a good three hours to work on a plan and try to get an answer or two before the other ladies arrived.

When I got in, the first thing I did was lock the door behind me and turn up the heat. I was done freezing to death. It was time to thaw out. Despite the heating in the car, my fingers were numb, and I couldn't feel my nose.

The sun rose higher in the sky, lending an orange-pink glow throughout the salon. I left the overhead lights off and only kept on the security lights that stay on all night and the Christmas lights. I never tired of those. There's even a string that hangs in the office. With those and the lamp, it was cozy and conducive to creative energy. And I needed all of that I could get.

I glanced at my watch. Someone should be at the coroner's office within the next hour. I grabbed a notepad from a drawer, ripped the top page off with a partial Paul Mitchell order written on it, and started jotting some things down.

Autopsy report.

Call Santa business to find out the name of Santa that was here for the festival.

Look into Della Birk.

Look into Trudy Flynn.

Get more info on Patti.

I studied my list as I tapped the pencil eraser on the desk, a habit that drove Claire insane. I had absolutely nothing to go on and no starting point except the unlikely hope of the autopsy report once the coroner's office opened. *Oh, where to start.* My stomach growled its answer. "With something from Stormi's supply of baked goods," I answered myself. Back out into the cold it was.

12

The grocery store was surprisingly busy. I hadn't anticipated so many people getting out in the cold unless they had to go to work. But I guess they could say the same thing about me. Except I would hope none of these people are investigating murders. *Sheesh!*

I headed straight for the bakery and was about halfway there when I came to two people, a man of about thirty-five in a stocking cap and Carhartt coat and a skinny bleached-blond woman of about the same age, with a black down coat. Tiny feathers poked through the shiny fabric.

"Hey," she said, her hand on my bicep. Her voice revealed years of smoking. "Aren't you the chick who owns the salon where they found the dead woman?"

I flinched. Is that how people recognized me now?

"You are!" she exclaimed before I could gather my wits about me. "I'm one of the people getting my haircut this afternoon. Think you could do it early since you're here anyway?"

"Um, no," I said. "No one is going to be there until one."

"But you're here already," she said. Lines around her eyes made her look years older than she probably was.

"I can't open for business before the rest of the ladies are there," I said. "Besides, I've got some things I need to get done before then." *Such as catch a killer.*

She drew back a bit and studied me, her lower lip between her teeth. "I guess it wouldn't be a good idea for us to be alone in the salon after—well, you know, after what happened and all." She bit her lower lip again, and her forehead puckered. "I mean—well, what if you're the one…"

Her blunt words took me back. She suspected that *I* might be the killer? "Well—I—What is your name?"

"Silver."

"Silver," I repeated and blinked with recognition. "You're actually one of my clients. I'm the one who called and left you the voicemail for the time to be at the salon. So I'll see you about one-thirty."

I hurried away before she could say another word. But I felt their gaze burning holes through me as I escaped as fast as I could.

I finally reached the bakery and opened the plexiglass case, going right for the blueberry and cream cheese-filled croissants. I grabbed it with the thin tissue paper when Stormi's face peered through the other side. I jumped back and laughed.

"Ah, a friendly face," I said.

"What's that mean?" she asked once she stopped laughing. "And why are you so jumpy?"

"Well, I just got recognized by some lady as 'the chick who owns the salon where they found the dead woman.'"

Stormi shrugged a shoulder. "At least she said *woman* as in singular. Which means she doesn't know about the first one a couple of years ago."

"Stormi!" I said before taking a deep breath and adding, "But you have a point."

She came around the counter and rubbed a couple of small circles on my upper back. "Just trying to make a bad situation better," she said. "Guess it was in poor taste, though, huh? My bad. Sorry."

I touched her arm briefly and shook my head. "Don't be sorry. I hate to say this, but I hope something big happens in this town, directing attention elsewhere. Wowzers! What are the chances that two people would drop in my salon?"

"What are you doing here on your day off?"

"We're finishing up the free haircuts this afternoon. Since we had to close early on the day of the festival, we didn't finish them all."

She looked at her watch and frowned. "But why are you here so early? You said you're finishing up this afternoon. That's not for several more hours."

"I had some things to do beforehand. Owning a business never leaves us without anything to do."

She made a snorting sound. "And you wonder why I haven't opened my own bakery yet."

I chuckled and reached into the soda cooler next to the counter and snatched a bottle of water. "See ya later, my friend." I turned to walk toward the checkout lanes.

"Hey, Mel?"

I turned around. "Yeah?"

"When are you and the ladies having your secret Santa reveal party?"

The last couple of years, Stormi had provided free pastries for our party, much to the ladies' delight.

"Evening after tomorrow."

"I've got a special treat for you all this year." I raised my eyebrows in interest. "I was in a Christmas cupcake baking contest. I made extras, and they're in my walk-in cooler. They're so dang cute if I have to say so myself." She grinned and puffed out her chest.

"That would be amazing! Thanks so much! Can I see them?"

"Come on back." She waved her hand, motioning for me to follow her. She opened the cooler, making sure it didn't shut tight behind us. "There," she said, pointing toward the back shelf.

"Oh, man! These are gorgeous!" I exclaimed. On a large silver platter were chocolate cupcakes with green swirled frosting to look like Christmas trees sitting on top. There were vanilla ones with mini marshmallows and green icing to look like a hat on top of a snowman's head with black pieces of candy for the eyes and mouth and a piece of orange candy for the nose. There were red velvet ones with white frosting and additional frosting in red, blue, yellow, and green that formed a string of lights swirled around on top. Though, my favorites were chocolate cupcakes with fluffy white frosting and had what looked like Santa's legs sticking out. "I wish I had your talent."

She beamed. "Yeah, I'm pretty proud of them."

"As well you should be!" I gave her a side hug. "But are you sure you want to give these away?"

"Yeah! What am I going to do with them? I can't eat them all."

I observed Santa's legs again and pointed to them, laughing. "That is such a clever idea. So creative."

"Thanks."

"Hey, just curious, do you know what company the plaza here uses to hire Santa for the festival?" I asked.

"No, but I can find out for you. Why?"

"Because when he spotted the police, he took off running, dumping a poor little boy sitting on his lap. Kind of odd behavior after a murder."

Stormi gasped. "Murder?"

I nodded. "You didn't see the paper this morning?" She shook her head. "Patti's death was ruled a homicide."

She shuddered and wrapped her arms around her middle. "That's creepy." She grabbed my arm and pulled me alongside her, a woman on a mission. "Come on. Let's ask the security guard. He'll know which company Santa came from."

"Do you know Della Birk?" I asked as we walked.

"Umm...I don't think so. I went to school with a Della, but her last name wasn't Birk. It was Lewis."

"Hmm."

We'd reached the front door where the security guard was scanning through his phone. Watching for shoplifters or anything else unsavvy wasn't on the top of his priority list. He glanced up when we neared and dropped his phone into his pocket as soon as he saw us. The name pin on his shirt said *Stan*.

"Hey, ladies," he said, suddenly all personality.

I wasn't sure I'd even noticed him before. What I noticed now, though, is how smitten he seemed with Stormi.

"Stan," she asked, "do you know who the Santa was for the festival?"

"Nope. Never saw him before. Why?"

"Just curious," I said. "Do you happen to know the name of the company that hires the Santa?"

He shrugged. "Sure. Star Lane Santa Company."

"From here in Birch Haven?" Stormi asked.

He shook his head. "Nah. On Star Lane in Oak Crest. Hence the name Star Lane Santa Company."

"Gotcha. Thanks, Stan," I said, turning to leave.

"Hey, Melanie," Stormi said, "let me know if there's anything I can do."

"You already have. And thanks."

"Sure thing. Come on down and get the cupcakes for your party. They'll hold for a few days in the freezer, but they won't be fresh, obviously. You know where they are if I'm not here."

"They'll be great! And thanks again."

On the walk back to the salon, I was quite satisfied. Not only had I gotten one of the town's best-baked goods, but I obtained one more string to unravel to solve the murder. It was going to be a good day.

13

The computer hummed to life as I twirled a strand of hair around my finger and bit my lower lip, anticipating another piece of information. When the screen popped up, I opened my search engine and typed in *Star Lane Santa Company, Oak Crest, MN*, and waited. Up popped a website with little Santa heads scattered across the background. At the forefront was information on hiring a Santa for a function, how to become a Santa with their company, the qualifications, and requirements and—wait! Santa school? There's such a thing? I couldn't decide if it was weird or cool. Rule number one should be *don't bolt from the police when you've got a child on your knee.*

Down at the bottom of the site was their contact information. I reached for my desk phone and punched in the number. I waited while it rang, exhaling long through pursed lips when an automated message came on. Darn it! *Ho! Ho! Ho! Thank you for calling Star Lane Santa Company. Please leave a message or call back during our business hours of ten to five. We look forward to making your event a memorable one.*

"Oh, our event was a memorable one, all right," I muttered as I hung up without leaving a voicemail. If I left a message, someone might not return my phone call until later. If I call back as soon as they open, I could probably talk to someone right away. I sat back and turned my wrist to see the face of my watch. Half an hour to go before I can call them back. But the coroner's office would be open by now.

I sat up straight again and searched for the phone number on my computer. It hadn't even completed one ring before someone answered.

"Tri-County Coroner's Office, can I help you?"

"Hi," I said. "I'm wondering if I can get a copy of an autopsy report? It was done yesterday."

I heard the clicking of keys on the other end. "Name?"

"Patti Parker."

"How are you related to the deceased?"

"Well—I—I'm not. But the reports are public record, are they not?" I crossed my fingers.

More clicking of keys, followed by throat clearing. "Under normal circumstances, yes."

"But?" I pressed, hoping for another nugget of information.

"I'm sorry, Ms—" She paused.

"Hogan. Melanie Hogan."

"Ms. Hogan, in cases where there is an ongoing investigation, the report cannot be released until the case is concluded."

I slumped in my chair. "Thank you," I said, less than enthusiastically. My emotions were on a rollercoaster ride that could challenge Disney's Space Mountain.

Twenty-four minutes left to go until Star Lane Santa Company opened. I drummed my fingertips on the desk and stared at nothing in particular before looking down at my list of people coming in today. There had been one person I hadn't been able to reach after three tries. Maybe once more was the charm.

I punched in the number, surprised when he answered. A success at this point was good, no matter how small. After setting the time, I hung up and passed the remaining minutes taking some inventory for the product supply companies coming by this week.

At ten o'clock sharp, I called Star Lane.

"Ho! Ho! Ho!" answered the woman. "And Merry Christmas to you and yours! How may we help you today?"

Her chipper attitude fit the role she was filling at the time, but I found it irritating. Proof that my nerves were a tad frayed.

"I'm hoping you can tell me who Santa was for the Birch Haven Christmas Festival on Saturday."

"His personal name?"

No, his Santa name. I rolled my eyes and forced a breath before answering. "Yes, his personal name. I'm assuming it wasn't Santa." I tried to sound like I was joking. I didn't want her to withhold information on account of my sarcasm. Anyone who knows me expects sarcasm. But it's not one of my finer traits in times such as these.

"I'm sorry, but I can't give out personal information."

"Can you tell me anything at all?" I pressed. "Anything."

It was quiet on her end of the phone line, and for a minute I thought I'd lost her.

"I can tell you that we didn't provide a Santa for the event," she said. "And that's all I can tell you."

My hope flailed. Had Stan given me the wrong company? Was I back to square one on this lead? "You're sure? That you didn't provide another Santa." I asked at the risk of making her more irritated than she was already becoming. *Someone wasn't very jolly for working with Santas all day,* I thought wryly.

"Of course I'm sure. The man who was supposed to be Santa was a no-show. Odd, too, since we'd never had a problem with him in the past," she mused, her tone a bit more friendly.

"And Star Lane didn't send a replacement?"

"We don't have enough Santa's to fill in at the drop of a hat. Especially this close to Christmas."

"And this man has never done this before? No-showed?"

"As I said, no. He's one of the most responsible men we have. And he's been with us for several years."

"Hmm." My mind was twirling in several directions. "You can't tell me his name?"

"I'm sorry, no."

"Has anyone checked on him to be sure he's okay?"

"Is there a reason you'd think he's not?" she asked, her tone sharper.

"No, no," I answered quickly. "Just that—well, you know."

"Ma'am, these things happen." The chirpiness of her voice had waned. "People get tired of the gig and just decide enough is enough. But listen, I've got other calls coming in. I have to run."

"One more thing," I rushed before she hung up. "Do you hire out elves, too?

"Sometimes. Mostly we're in the Santa business, though. Bye, now."

"Did you—" The line went dead. After a few seconds of holding the receiver, I hung it up. If the scheduled Santa didn't show, then who was the impromptu Santa? And had the fraud done something terrible with the original one? I had to find out who it was and pay him a visit. *To make sure he was okay*, I told myself, validating the nosiness. But first, I needed to find out who the guy was. And how was I going to do that?

I scanned my list on the desk and jotted a brief summary next to *Santa*. So far, the Santa fraud, Della the elf, and Trudy were my main suspects. Santa and elf were on the list because of their strange behavior, taking off from the police. And Trudy was suspicious because of her confrontation with Patti before the murder. Even though, technically, it was Patti who threatened Trudy. Still, it was a well-known fact that the person threatened or bullied could lash out at their tormentor if it had gone on long enough. Maybe Trudy was fed up.

I finished up with some inventory and bookwork before the ladies all trailed in within a half-hour of each other. Claire was the first to arrive. I was looking at the appointment book for the upcoming week when she came in, looking a little ragged. She was usually the most put-together person I knew, looking like a model even when she put on sweatpants or yoga pants.

"Sweetie, are you okay?" I asked the minute I saw her.

"Yeah, why?" Her smile didn't quite reach her eyes.

"It's me, Claire." I strode to the front of the desk, looped my arm through hers, and guided her back to the office. "Don't take this the wrong way, but you don't look so hot."

She laughed softly. Another unusual behavior for Claire. She was always happy and laughed a lot, but never softly. Her laugh was genuinely joyous and infectious. Not soft.

"Well, I'm not sure how to take that," she said.

"Fill me in. What's going on?"

She met my gaze with one that looked like she'd been up all night. "I'm a suspect in a murder investigation. Isn't that enough?"

"Person of interest," I teased lightly, attempting to make her feel a little better. If even for a moment.

"Okay, police officer," she attempted to tease back in a voice that lacked spark. "I had to go to the station before I came here."

My eyes grew wide. "Why didn't you call me? I would have met you there."

"There's nothing you could have done, Mel." She straightened her skirt, then her headscarf, both white with little green wreaths throughout. At least she was still dressing normally. And she wasn't wearing an orange jumpsuit. Yet.

"I could have been there for support." I felt the cold sting of being left out of such an important piece of the process. "You didn't have to be alone. Oh!" I exclaimed, "Cole was there, right? So you weren't alone." It was a statement rather than a question.

"No."

"No?" I frowned and grabbed her arm. "Claire, why—"

"I didn't call him. I can't have him involved in this, Mel. I've already caused him enough trouble." She reminded me of that little phone emoji of the face with the large, sad eyes.

I put my arm around her waist and pulled her in for a side hug. She smelled of Irish Spring and peach. "Hun, you fetched Patti a cup of coffee. That's hardly the cause of any trouble Cole may have. Besides, he's banned from the investigation. He can't be banned from you, too, for crying out loud."

She sighed. "Better safe than sorry."

She plopped down in the chair, and I took the other.

"Walker?" I asked.

She squinted. "What?"

"Was it Walker who talked with you?"

"Oh! Yes. He's nice enough, I suppose."

"Nice is good and all, but is he competent?" I contemplated telling her what I'd been up to. I didn't want to get her hopes up, but I wanted her to know we would clear her. "Santa was a fraud," I blurted.

She chuckled, almost sounding genuinely amused. "You just now discovered he's not real?"

"I mean the Santa that bolted when he saw Cole the day of the festival. He was a fraud. The real Santa never showed up." I told her what I'd found out from Star Lane Santa Company. "Did you know there's such a thing as Santa school?"

"No, sir," she said, laughing.

"Yes, sir." I nodded emphatically. "Anyway, I've got my whiteboard out."

Rubie turned the corner. "That whiteboard is getting lots of good use from you."

Claire and I both startled. We'd been so deep in thought we hadn't even heard the door.

"Connie's here, too," Rubie said. "Babs was right behind us. What are you guys talking about so seriously?"

"I had to go to the police station before coming here to give a more detailed statement," Claire said.

Connie came around the corner and joined us as Babs hollered out from the front. "Happy free service day!" Her voice got louder as she neared the office. "Whoa! Why so serious?" she asked when she saw us.

"Claire had to go to the police station to give a statement," Rubie said.

Rubie looked like she was going to be sick. Connie, too, for that matter.

"What's got the two of you?" I asked. "You both look like you just ate something terrible. Like pickled pigs' feet."

"Gross!" Rubie squealed and gave me a dirty look. "Why would you even say that?"

"I just feel terrible for mentioning that you got coffee for Patti," Connie said. "I can't forget about it." Her voluptuous frame filled the doorway. "Geez." She shook her head slowly. Babs was on her tiptoes, peering over Connie's shoulder.

"Me, too," Rubie said. "Seriously. Why can't I ever just keep my mouth shut."

"Ladies, come on," I said. "Let's be realistic. It's not like they wouldn't have found out. And it's not like you did it intentionally or maliciously."

"Change of subject please," Claire said, crossing one long leg over the other at the knee. She brushed something invisible from her green tights.

"Where do you ladies want to do the Secret Santa reveal this year?" I asked.

"Why wouldn't we do it here like we always do?" Connie asked.

I shrugged. "I just thought with everything that's happened, you might want to take it somewhere else."

Claire shook her head. "Uh-uh. I want to do it here. I want good memories to push away the bad."

I nodded. "Deal. Wednesday after work still good for everyone?"

"Totally!"

"Yup!"

"I'm in!" they all said in unison.

"Everyone called the people on their list for today, right?" I asked.

"Oh, shoot!" Rubie exclaimed, her hand over her mouth. "I knew I forgot to do something!"

I gave her a sidelong glance, then shook my head slowly. "For real?"

"No." She grinned. "I'm blond, but I'm not dumb."

I chuckled. Leave it to Rubie. "If anyone hears anything in the way of Patti's death, let me know. In fact, if anything sounds at all suspicious or helpful, anything," I stressed. "Please, please, please, ask questions whenever you can."

"We get it," Rubie said. "We'll scream it from the rooftops."

"My guess is we'll hear something since all of these people were here the day of the death," Babs said. "Heck, we might even solve this thing by the end of the day." She hiked up the waist of her pants that had fallen low on her narrow hips.

I scoffed. "If only it were that easy."

Suddenly someone yanked on the locked door, followed by a knock.

"Show's on, ladies," I said, winking at Claire.

"Let's do this," she said.

14

Most of my older clientele were 'blue-hairs,' the nickname we affectionately gave the generation of women who liked a blue rinse added to their yellow-gray hair before setting. It counteracts the yellow and gives their hair a silver-blue color. It was popular in Britain in the thirties and appears it will continue. I'd never liked it much, but who knows, I might be one someday.

But my first client this afternoon, Millie, was an elderly woman with long, naturally silver hair worn in a single braid just like my grandmother. But when Millie began talking, the similarities ended there. I had to keep myself from laughing out loud as she cussed a streak bluer than my blue-hairs at the inconvenience of having to come back.

"There's no reason why ya couldn't a done it Saturday, dontcha know. It's not like the dead woman was a comin' back ta life, and she sure as hell wasn't gettin' any deader."

She said this with expletives laced throughout that I wouldn't be caught dead saying. And she had all eyes and ears in the room, some wide with horror and some trembling with repressed laughter.

"And that Santa! Why in Sam Hill they get a new one? He was a joke, dontcha know. Didn't even stick around the afternoon. He up and left." Again, her sentence was laced with expletives, making crystal clear just how much she disapproved of Mr. Fraud Claus.

"Who was Santa before this year?" I asked.

"Nick Frost!" she exclaimed. "You didn't know that? Why Nick's been the Santa around these parts far back as I remember. Hope he didn't up and die, dontcha know." She clucked, and I stopped my shears in mid-cut as she shook her head. "Shame if he did, uh-huh. He was a good 'un."

I peered into the mirror and caught Claire's gaze. We shared a look of triumph. This afternoon was shaping up to be quite successful even though we were all basically working for nothing.

"How well do you know Nick Frost?" I asked. The irony of his name hadn't escaped me. It had to be a fake name. That or his mother named him with a specific profession in mind—Santa school.

"Know him enough to know he wouldn't a left before the party was over." She clucked again. "Shame."

"Is he from Birch Haven?" I asked.

She turned her head to look at me and narrowed her eyes. "He's too old for you, child. And he doesn't have any money I know of, so don't be gettin' any ideas."

I snickered, and she turned forward again. "He lives on the outskirts of town somewheres. East, I believe."

Thankfully I finished with my shears without any casualties from Millie turning her head every which way while she talked. I lay them down and picked up the blow dryer.

"Put that dern thing away," she said, swatting at my hand. "I'm no sissy. Just braid it, and I'm off."

I lay my hand on her shoulder. "Millie, it's freezing cold out there. Let me dry it first, and then I'll braid it." Styling wasn't part of our free services, but it would take me all of two minutes.

"Oh, fine," she conceded.

She was quiet during the blow-dry, thank goodness. If she talked over the blow dryer's noise, her colorful language would have been heard clear down the way.

As soon as Millie left, I darted for the office, dug my notepad out from under the desk blotter, and wrote *Santa Nick Frost — lives on the Eastern outskirts of BH*. Not that it's an easy name to forget, but one never knows what I might forget by the end of this crazy day.

My next appointment, the skinny bleached blond from the grocery store whose name escaped me, was a no-show. I considered waiting a few minutes in case she arrived late. Maybe she'd decided against letting a possible killer near her head with a sharp object. Rather than wait, I decided to see if my next appointment had arrived early. If so, bleached blond would have to wait.

I strode over toward the waiting area where six people absently flipped through magazines. Well, five of them were flipping. The sixth was a teenager so engrossed in what she was reading I doubted she would notice if the Christmas tree fell on top of her. The *Seventeen* magazine was about two inches from her face. Green framed glasses were perched upon a button nose. I smiled and scanned the little area.

"Toni?" I said, watching for one of the six to acknowledge my call. No one moved. "Toni?" I said louder.

"Toni!" The woman sitting next to the girl, most likely mom, said as she tapped the side of the girl's knee with the back of her hand. "You're next," she said.

The girl looked up, her glasses riding low on the bridge of her nose. "What?" she said, looking about her.

"You're next," the woman repeated. "Go!" She tapped the girl's knee again, harder this time.

Toni pushed her glasses up with one finger and dropped the magazine on her mother's lap. I led her back to my chair, affixed a tissue neck strip, and whisked a cape around her, fastening the Velcro around her neck.

"Must have been a good magazine," I said, grinning at her through the mirror.

"Yeah." She gave me a small smile, revealing braces with neon green rubber bands.

"Green's your favorite color, I bet, huh?" I ran my hands through her long hair. "So, what are we going to do today?"

"Mom!" she called over toward the waiting room, turning the heads of every mother in the salon. "Bring me that magazine."

Oh, no. This cut was going to be tricky. Most people who wanted their hair like a photo they've seen don't realize that the style will not look the same as it does in the picture. Hair texture, facial shape and features, cowlicks, they all were critical factors. When I saw the photo Toni held in front of me now, I knew this was one of those times. Toni and the girl in the picture couldn't look more different.

I pulled my fingers through the sides of her hair. "I can cut it like it is in the photo, but I have to tell you it won't look like the photo."

"Why not?" she said with a touch of attitude.

"Your hair is very fine, and the girl in the photo has extremely thick hair. And it looks like the girl in this photo has naturally wavy hair."

"But I want my hair like that," she complained.

"Who doesn't?" her mother said, now by her side. Mom rolled her eyes. "Toni, you can't always have what you want. We've been through this before. Every time Jenny gets her hair cut, you want yours the same way. Jenny's hair is thick and wavy like this picture."

"Mom," she complained, her disappointment apparent.

"You are your own person, honey," mom said. "Find your own hairstyle without trying to copy Jenny."

I listened carefully, the name getting my attention.

"Jenny?" I asked.

"She's my best friend," Toni said, smiling like she'd just won a popularity contest.

Mom rolled her eyes again and shook her head. "Jenny is the girl the rest of the girls want to be like because she's pretty. But trust me, it's outside only." She thrust her thumb toward her chest. "Not so much inside."

Toni's chin jutted outward. "Jenny's mom lets her do whatever she wants with her hair." She cast an accusatory glance toward her mother.

"Maybe Jenny's mom doesn't care as much as your mom," I offered gently. Her mom smiled her thank you. "By chance, does Jenny have dark hair and about fourteen years old?" I knew the odds weren't high, with Jenny being such a common name and all, but it didn't hurt to ask. I was on a roll today. And, after all, as Babs stated earlier, all of these people were here on the day of the festival.

"Yeah," Toni said.

"Was she here Saturday for the festival?"

"Uh-uh," Toni said. "I was supposed to meet her here, but I never saw her." I felt my hopes dash a bit. I figured it was too good to be true, but trying didn't hurt.

"What is this Jenny's last name?" I asked.

"Landis or something like that," her mother answered. "Jenny Landis. Linus. L something or other. And she's a pistol," she added under her breath.

"I heard that, Mom," Toni said with another accusatory look. "You don't know her. You don't like any of my friends."

Toni's mother shook her head slowly and wandered back toward the waiting area. *Silent Night* piped through the speakers in the ceiling. I had a feeling it wouldn't be a silent night in Toni's house.

"So tell me about Jenny," I said as casually as possible.

"Why?" Toni asked. "So you can take my mom's side?"

"On the contrary. I would never come between friends. But it might not be a bad idea to understand that your mom has her opinions just as you have yours. And hers are probably based on wanting the best for you." *Unlike my own mother.* "What's Jenny's mom's name?"

"I dunno." She shrugged a shoulder. "Never met her. I don't think her and Jenny have the same last name, though. I just know her mom's super cool. She lets Jenny do whatever she wants because she trusts her."

I noticed a bitter twist on the word *trust*.

"What's Jenny's last name?" I asked, holding my breath. She hadn't said it when I asked her mom a moment ago, but surely she had to know it if she thought this girl was all that.

"Why?"

Goodness! So much attitude for one word.

"Just curious if I know her or not." It wasn't exactly a lie. Not really.

"Probably not."

I took a breath. "You know, Toni," I said, "really cool moms care what their kids are doing."

She peered at me through the mirror. "Did yours?"

"Nope." The resentment I thought I'd shed months back pricked at me again. "That's how I know."

"Well, Jenny's mom let her come alone last Saturday."

"I thought you said Jenny wasn't here."

"Yeah, but she *could have come* alone if she'd wanted to." She rolled her eyes, clearly irritated with my inability to understand her point. "My mom had to be right by my side the whole time. It was obnoxious."

"How old is Jenny?" I asked. "Same age as you?"

"Yeah. Fourteen."

157

"What'd you say her last name was again?"

"I didn't." She narrowed her eyes at me. "But it's Buckley. You're sure interested in Jenny. What'd she do?"

"Nothing that I know of. Just making conversation." I lay a hand lightly on her shoulder and raised an eyebrow as I held her gaze in the mirror. "But to be honest, if it were my child, I wouldn't let her run around on her own in town at that age."

"But her mom trusts her," she argued.

"And unless you've given her reason not to, I'll bet your mom trusts you, too. It's other people that are not always trustworthy." I thought about Patti's killer running around out there somewhere. "There are shady characters where you would least expect them."

The look in her eyes softened a bit. "I guess I hadn't thought of that."

"Your mom cares enough about you to want you to stay safe." I gave her a gentle smile.

The envy returned to her eyes just as quickly as I'd made any headway.

"She needs to trust that I could handle myself if someone tried to hurt me. We're learning self-defense in PE class at school." The attitude returned.

Recognizing a lost battle, I smiled and continued cutting her hair in silence. Jenny wasn't a high priority in this case. She had been a person of interest in my initial investigation, but at this point, she was of little interest.

15

The next couple of hours went quickly as we each took person after person back to our stations. There was no time to bother looking at the clock. It wouldn't have mattered. We had our lineup and wouldn't quit until we finished. And by the looks of things, not a single one of us—including me— obtained any more information, despite questioning our clients as much as possible without making them run for the door. *Did you know Patti Parker? What were you doing last Saturday between one and two? Do you come to the festival every year? Were you outside when Santa bolted? What about when the elf did? Do you know either of them?* And on and on we quizzed and fired questions, listening to anything that might have been useful in between. A couple of the ladies thought they had a few bites, but none panned out.

At a little after four-twenty, I looked up as a blast of cold air followed in the bleached blond scheduled to be here hours ago.

"Remember me? Silver. Can you fit me in?" she called over to me.

I felt a sliver of irritation. "It will be a while," I said. "You were scheduled at 1:30."

"That's why I wanted to come earlier," she said. "When I saw you at the grocery store. Because I knew I had to run a couple of errands for my best friend's wedding. It got moved up at the last minute, and my regular stylist couldn't fit me in for two weeks. I was a little panicked when I couldn't get in on Saturday. But I guess a murder is a good reason to close early."

I hesitated and tightened my lips before an annoyed retort could escape. It would be nice to take a good six inches off from her frizzed, stringy hair.

"I'm running ahead so I can squeeze her in," Claire offered before I'd decided.

"Oh, thank you so much! You have no idea how much I appreciate this!" Silver gushed. "The wedding is Wednesday evening, and one of my errands was getting my dress fitted."

"I love weddings!" Rubie added to the conversation, positively beaming.

She loved them as much as I disliked them. It's not so much I disliked marriage or weddings in general, just an entire day making small talk with strangers. Yuck! It exhausted me. But if there was a white wedding cake involved, it was worth it.

"Who's getting married?" Rubie asked from across the salon.

"Della. She said to ask for you," she said to Rubie. "But beggars can't be choosers, as they say."

That's probably where I'd heard the name before, I thought.

"Yeah!" Rubie exclaimed. "I was supposed to do her hair for the wedding, but then she canceled, telling me the date had changed."

I turned my client's chair as I whisked the cape from around her neck. I looked at Silver. "Well, I'm not Rubie, but I can take care of you in just a moment."

"Oh, you're a doll," she said as she slipped her coat off and hung it on the coat tree.

"Hey, Claire," I said as I led my client up to the front counter. "Can you maybe grab my next one instead?" I took a few steps toward Claire on my way up front and murmured, "It's a man's haircut, so it should be speedy."

She gave me an odd look. "Sure. Why?"

"Trust me on this. Besides, the guy hasn't a clue who was scheduled to cut his hair anyway."

She shrugged a shoulder. "Sure."

After sending my client out the door, I hustled back to my station, dumped the comb and brush from my last client into the jar of Barbicide, sprayed down my counter and shears, then swept the hair on the floor.

"Come on back, Silver," I said, whisking the cape from the back of my chair.

She sat down, the smell of stale cigarettes making my stomach turn. I fastened the paper neck strip, then the cape.

"Can I smoke in here? My regular stylist lets me smoke." She shoved a hand in her purse and pulled out a box of Marlboros.

I stared at her in disbelief for a moment. Smoking inside public buildings has been illegal everywhere for quite a while now.

"That would be a no." I envisioned us all going up in flames. "Fire and flammables don't mix so well." I narrowed an eye and looked at her through the mirror. "Where is the salon you normally go to?"

"Oh, it's not a joint like you have here. It's in her house. She's on vacation for two weeks so this free gig turned out good."

I shook my head, clearing my bewilderment. I sure hoped the woman had a good insurance policy. "So, what are we doing today?"

"Just a trim," she said, dropping the pack of cigarettes back into her purse.

My dream of cutting inches flew away. "Did you want to look at a styling book for some ideas?" I asked, hopefully.

"Not this time. With the wedding, I can't do anything too drastic. Della would kill me."

I swallowed my disappointment. "Of course. Let's go back to the shampoo bowls." I led her back, got her comfortable, and began running the water. "So, Della's getting married?" I asked.

"Yeah. You know her?"

I shook my head. "No. Just that she was the elf for the Christmas Festival last Saturday."

"She's awesome," Rubie chirped from her station. She paused from combing through a shoulder-length bob cut to chat. "Don't you remember when she brought in all those to-die-for bagels for us from her brother's birthday breakfast at Bagel Haven?" Rubie asked.

I raised my hand in the air. "That's right!" I exclaimed. "She brought in enough to feed the entire town! She had on the glasses with the super cute blue frames."

"I knew she was getting married, but I didn't know the reason she canceled me is because it got moved up so soon," Rubie said.

"She probably thought it would have been too short notice for you," Silver said to Rubie. "Things kinda ramped up when her husband-to-be got a job out of state. Her brother wanted her married here and not where they're moving. He—her brother, not the one she's marrying—was the dude ringing the bell for the festival. Him and Della have always been close."

"Who is she marrying?" I asked.

"Guy by the name of Donny West. Super good guy."

I glanced at Rubie, who shrugged. "Never heard of him," Rubie said.

"Me either," I said. I draped a towel over Silver's freshly washed hair and led her back to my station. As I combed through her wet hair, I asked, "Silver, do you know why Della would run away if she saw the police?"

"Nope."

"Did she know Patti Parker?"

"The dead woman?" Silver asked. She regarded me skeptically. "If you're asking if Della would have killed that woman, no. Absolutely not! Della's got a bit of a colorful past, but she's no killer."

"Did she know Patti?" I asked again.

"You'd have to ask her that. I'd say no, though. Don't know where she'd ever have met someone like her."

"Someone like her?" I asked.

She cocked her head to the side and looked at me through the mirror. "It's no secret the woman was a nightmare. It's all over town. But I'm tellin' ya, Della wouldn't hurt anyone. She's got the softest heart of anyone I know. She can't stand to see people hurt."

"About the colorful past you mentioned—"

"It's not my place to talk about Della's life," she said. "She's a good lady who's finally got her poop in a group. She's got a good man and making a decent life for herself."

I nodded and combed through the rest of the tangles as I contemplated getting more information. Silver so much as said talking about Della was over. But she certainly wasn't done talking altogether. Her incessant chatter continued non-stop, getting louder when I started blow-drying her hair.

When I finished, I thanked her and wished her well at the wedding.

"Just so you know," she said as I sent her on her way, "I wouldn't upset Della before her wedding by being nosy about her past. Her brother is pretty protective of her. I wouldn't want to see you get hurt. If you know what I mean."

Before I could say another word, Silver was out the door, slipping an arm into the sleeve of her coat as she trotted to her car.

Claire's head snapped around to look in my direction, and our eyes met. That was certainly an interesting turn of events.

"Exactly how protective is Della's brother?" I muttered to Claire as I passed her.

She raised an eyebrow in answer.

I strode to the office and jotted down my newly acquired information on my notepad, flipped it facedown, and proceeded to take my next client back.

The last hour felt like five hours. All I could think about was what I'd found out since this morning, turning all kinds of scenarios around in my head. I ran some of them by Claire.

"Instead of my house this evening, let's go to Grizzley's Tap House for dinner," I said to Claire after our last clients left. Babs finished early and had already left for the day. Rubie and Connie were finishing up their last.

"I'll have to see if the sitter can stay a little longer," she said.

"How about we see if Nana wants to spend some time with her. They're good for each other."

"They are," she said, her smile lighting up her whole face. "Of course, Rose is good for anyone."

Affectionate warmth spread over me. "Yeah, she is. If you're in, I'll call her."

"I'm in," Claire said. "Call your grandmother, and I'll let Rubie know."

Grizzley's Tap House is our favorite place, and we meet there at least every other week. They know us there, they like us, and they always manage to land us our favorite booth.

***

A mere hour later, Claire, Rubie, and I were tucked away in our favorite corner booth at Grizzley's. The festive atmosphere helped ease the seriousness we felt about solving this murder and clearing Claire. Laughter filled the air, and for a moment, it was easy to forget everything else. Only for a moment.

Multi-colored Christmas lights adorned every wall, and Christmas music blasted overhead. Lighted Christmas ornaments hung in the windows. Nature even added to the festive mood as the bitter cold frosted the windows making shapes that appeared like snowflakes. Men and women alike sported brown reindeer antler headbands adorned with holly, and some wore Santa hats. Mistletoe hung in the doorway leading to the kitchen and another sprig above the bar.

"Sydney's with Rose?" Rubie asked Claire, her voice rising above the music and laughter.

"Yeah." She smiled, and her eyes warmed. "I'm not sure who enjoys it more, Syd or Rose."

"Definitely my grandmother," I said. Watching the two of them together melted my heart. And I knew how Syd felt because it was how I felt every day when I came home from school. When I slipped through the door, and the kitchen's aromas greeted me, it was like entering heaven day after day. Even when Nana worked as a nurse at the hospital, she was never too busy for me. The memories changed my mind. "Syd," I said. "Syd has to enjoy it more."

The server, Angie, arrived at our table, chatted for a few minutes, and slapped a cocktail napkin down in front of each of us. "What'll it be, ladies," she asked. "Same? We have some Christmas cocktails available if you want to switch it up a bit. Even a new pink one for you, Rubie," she said.

"Well then," Rubie said joyfully, "I'll have one of those."

"You don't even know what it is yet," I said and grinned.

"Does it matter?" she said. "It's pink. Not all of us need to plan everything out."

Claire and Angie laughed.

"She's got a point, Melanie," Angie said.

I pressed my lips together as I thought about my order and said, "I'll have my usual."

"Of course you will," Rubie said, disapproval obvious."

After we'd added our food order, Angie bounced away.

"Just once, I'd love to see you do something spontaneous," Rubie said.

Claire groaned and covered her eyes with a hand. "Oh, don't say that." She peeked at Rubie through two slightly separated fingers. "I wish you could have known her before she suddenly decided she wanted some spontaneity in her life."

"No, thank you," Rubie said. "Boring!"

It hadn't been more than a few years ago that I led a quiet, stable, well-planned life. If it had been possible, I would have even planned my bathroom breaks. All this to be as unlike my birth mother as humanly possible. Until one day something nudged me to want some excitement in my life. And I got it— in dead bodies. But I'd also discovered I was pretty good at this investigation stuff. I told Levi he should get me hired on as a detective with the Birch Haven Police Department before someone else snaps me up. But he shot that down quickly. He didn't even think about it before he said no. In fact, he didn't just say 'no,' he said, 'hell no.' How rude. I chuckled at the memory.

"What?" Rubie asked me.

I startled. "Huh?"

"What are you finding so amusing?"

I told her about Levi's response to my suggestion. "He could have at least pretended to entertain the idea," I said, grimacing. "Insulting."

"The guy's smart, not an idiot." Claire giggled.

"Very funny. I need another napkin," I said as I spread my cocktail napkin out and snagged a pen from my purse. "My notebook stayed on my desk. This napkin has just become a makeshift whiteboard."

16

"So here's what we know so far," I began, writing on the napkin as I spoke. "The originally scheduled Santa failed to appear." I looked at each of them and pushed a chunk of hair out of my eyes. "According to the company he worked for, that's something he's never done before."

"We should look into that," Rubie said, chewing on her gum, then blowing a pink bubble.

"I've already started. Kind of. I at least found out his name, Nick Frost, and a general idea of where he lives."

"Isn't there an actor with the name Nick Frost?" Rubie asked.

I shrugged. "Probably. People in show biz change their names to all kinds of weird ones. But this isn't Hollywood."

"I can't help but wonder if that's his real name," Claire said. "I mean, come on. How could that happen organically? Unless his mother is some kind of psychic and knew what he would do with his life."

I frowned. "I sure hope not. How heartbreaking for a mother to know at her child's birth that his dream would be to play Santa when he grew up."

"Can we say underachiever?" Rubie said, flipping her blond ponytail over her shoulder.

"Not everyone aspires to be a highfalutin tootin' hairstylist," I said, which earned me a harsh squint.

"Seriously," Claire said. "We may need to consider that Nick Frost isn't his real name."

"Of course I'll look into that," I said. "And then we have Trudy Flynn." I wrote her name on the napkin and looked up at the ladies. "Either of you know anything about her?"

"Nothing."

"Nada."

They both answered at the same time.

"I'll see what I can find out. If she grew up around here, it shouldn't be too hard," I said.

"I'd think one of us would know her from the salon if she's from around here," Rubie said.

I grinned at her. "Hate to break it to you, sister, but not everyone in Birch Haven comes to our salon. We're not the only game in town."

Rubie shrugged. "The only one worth playing. And if she was coming to our salon, even the one time, it proves she wasn't happy with her current stylist."

"Some people will do anything to get something for free," I countered. "Even betray their stylist."

Claire picked up her phone and started tapping, then scrolling. "Trudy Flynn. Here she is on Facebook."

I scooted over close to her and watched as she scrolled through the friends on Trudy's Facebook page. I was just about to lean back again when Patti's picture popped up.

"What?" I squawked. "Patti and Trudy were Facebook friends?"

"Right?" Claire said. "Hard to understand since they appeared to dislike each other so much."

I drew back slightly and raised my eyebrows. "*Dislike*? It's okay to say *hate* in this circumstance, Claire."

"I don't think they *hated* each other, Mel. Maybe they were just going through a difficult season."

"I'd say," Rubie scoffed then blew another bubble.

Angie appeared at our table with our drinks. She went to set mine down but set it back on the tray before slapping another napkin down first. "Playing detective again?" she asked me when she saw the scribbling on the once-white napkin laid on the table before me.

I smiled innocently. "Just helping the police do their job."

175

"And I'm sure they appreciate it." Angie chuckled and hurried away to another table.

I glanced at Rubie's drink and shivered as I imagined the sickening sugary sweetness.

Rubie took a sip and looked at Claire. "If Angie knew you were a suspect, she'd have set her tray down and helped us."

"Well, we don't need anyone else knowing about that," Claire said with a sigh.

I tapped the napkin with my pointer finger. "Let's get back to it. Claire, see what you can find on Patti's Facebook page."

"Just a sec," she said, looking at the screen. "I'm still looking at Trudy's."

"Who had Trudy on their call list to come back in this afternoon?" I asked.

"I did," Rubie said. "But it was a wrong number."

"Do you still have the list on you?" I asked. "Maybe you punched the number in wrong."

"Yes, because I wouldn't have checked it against the number dialed," she said flippantly before taking another drink.

I dropped my chin slightly and looked up at her. "Slow down on that thing, or I'll be carrying you home."

"Like you could, you little shrimp." She chuckled.

"Could you humor me and double-check? Pretty please?" I pleaded.

"Yeah, yeah." She shook her head slowly and picked up her phone. "I didn't clear any of the numbers after calling, so I know it's one of them. I can look and see how much time I spent on each outgoing call. Most of the ones I spoke with will be longer."

I watched as both of them disappeared into the electronic world of endless information. Claire and I were seated on the same side of the booth, so I leaned over again to look at her screen then pointed to it.

"Stormi is a friend of Trudy's?"

"It appears," Claire said absently. "So Trudy went to Birch Haven High School, graduating with the class of 2007." She fiddled a bit more then said, "Same with Patti."

"I'll look up Patti's page," I said as I grabbed my phone and got to work.

Claire and I scrolled through pictures on each of their sites while Rubie studied the recent call list on her phone.

"Wait!" I exclaimed. "Here's a photo of a high-school-aged Patti with a boy in a Birch Haven Wolves football uniform." I moved it closer to my face. "This kid looks an awful lot like the man in Trudy's recent photos. It's a young version of Trudy's husband."

"Which means Patti used to date Trudy's husband," Claire said. "That puts a whole new spin on things."

"Right?" I said. "People kill over love every day."

"Let me see!" Rubie said, setting aside her phone.

"What's his name?" I asked Claire, reaching over and scrolling to the relationship status where it revealed, *Married to Norman Flynn*. I jotted his name down next to Trudy's, drew a line between the two, and wrote *husband/wife* on the line.

"Let's ask Stormi about them tomorrow since she's Facebook friends with Trudy. She may be able to shed light on some of this." I wrote *Stormi* under the possible suspect list on the napkin.

"Oh, come on!" Rubie exclaimed when she saw me. "You're listing Stormi as a suspect?"

"Sure," I said. "She knew Patti. I'm not ruling anyone out." I nudged Claire's shoulder with my own. "Except you." I turned my attention back to the napkin, tapped my finger on it, and said, "And then we have Della's brother. Howard was it?"

"Yup," Claire said.

"Apparently he's super protective of Della. Exactly *how* protective is the question," I said.

"Other than going to the same school, what's the connection between Patti and Della?" Rubie asked. "As far as I know, Della is a sweetheart."

"Clients don't always tell their stylist everything," I said, meeting Rubie's eyes. "Maybe she has deep-seated secrets you know nothing about."

Rubie shuddered, blinking her big blue eyes. "Freaky. But I still can't imagine it. Even still, how are you connecting her to Patti's death?"

"I don't know yet," I said, tapping the pen on the table. "Other than the two of them were both there at the same time. And innocent people don't run when they see the police."

Rubie shrugged. "Good point. But she's a sweetheart, I'm telling ya."

"Uh-huh," I said with an eye roll. Anyone can be who they need to be for short periods. Eventually, their true colors show, though. "I need to find out more about Della's brother."

"Let's crash her wedding. Della's," she said.

I gasped and high-fived her. "Genius!"

"Count me out," Claire said. "I have my baby girl, and I'm not getting her in the middle of this. Plus, I'm already away from her tonight."

"Me and Mel will go," Rubie said. "Della has been talking about her wedding for months and months."

"Instead of us crashing it, call her and offer your services," I suggested. "Let her know you found out about the change in plans."

"Duh!" she said, making a face at me. She grabbed her phone, scrolled through her contacts, and tapped the name. Claire and I both watched her.

"Della?" she said, smiling. "This is Rubie. Hey, one of your bridesmaids was in the salon this afternoon. She said you moved up your wedding to this week." She listened a moment and then said, "Yeah, that's why I'm calling. I'd be happy to." She gave us a thumbs up and grinned. "Yup," she said. "Okay, see you then."

She ended the call and set her phone on the table, then grinned at me. "I'm in. I have to be there at five-fifteen."

"Sounds good. I'll be sure I'm available if any of her attendants need help with their hair."

She studied me, her face as innocent as a spring day. "You should just come with me when I go there, in case you want to nose around—I mean, help out with hair."

I gave her a half-smile. "I'll do that."

"But remember that this is her wedding day. Don't blow it for her."

I put my hand to my chest and opened my eyes wide. "Me? I wouldn't do that."

"Not intentionally," she said, "but that doesn't mean it won't happen. I'm only doing this so you can find out for yourself that Della is not the killer."

"Proving Claire's innocence is more important to me than Della's wedding," I said. Then added, "Getting the person who murdered in my salon is, too."

I picked up my phone and opened Della's social media page.

"What are you looking for now?" Claire asked.

"Someone by the name of Howard so I can see what he looks like and get the last name."

"Della's not married yet, so it should be the same as hers," Rubie said.

I shook my head as I searched the screen. "Not necessarily. Della may have been married before, they may have different fathers or different mothers, they may—"

"I get it," Rubie said, holding up a hand.

Angie appeared with our food, setting plates down in front of Rubie and Claire. She held mine a few feet above me, waiting for me to move the napkin, filled with writing by now.

"Heard of paper?" she asked me.

"Didn't have any on me," I said, moving the napkin.

She smiled, set the plate down, and hurried off to the next table.

"Here's a guy by the name of Howard," I said, zooming in closer on the photo. "Doesn't say anything about being family, though."

"Let me see," Claire said. I lay my phone in her outstretched hand. "I think this is the guy that was ringing the bell in front of the grocery store," she said, using her thumb and forefinger to stretch the photo bigger. "And someone did say her brother was the bell ringer."

"Are you sure this is the guy?" I asked.

She studied closer. "Yup. I remember because he was acting a little weird."

"Weird as in how?" Rubie asked.

"Not sure. Just that it caught my attention."

"Try to remember," I said. "Anything at all." I watched as she chewed on her lower lip, concentrating hard.

"I think it was just that he was more interested in what was going on around him than doing his thing with the bell and the kettle for the money. Someone could have come and swiped the entire kettle, and I don't think he would have known it happened."

I scrunched up my nose. "Not much to go on there, girl. I'll find some reason to talk with him at Della's wedding. Once I have a little more info on all of these people, I can start working on their motives."

"Are you going to tell Levi any of this?" Rubie asked.

"Any of what?" I said.

17

On my way home from Grizzley's Tap House, I called Levi.

"Hey, Blondie," he answered on the first ring.

His playful tone reminded me his son Jackson was there tonight. And it amazed me what the sound of his voice could do to me, no matter what tone he conveyed.

"Sitting on your phone, or what?" I asked.

"Jackson and I are playing a game of Monopoly."

"He's winning, I bet, huh?" I asked.

"Of course. Wish you were here with us. We might even let you win," he said.

"Hi, Melanie!" hollered a young voice. "Dad's cheating again!"

I grinned as I pictured the two of them sitting at the kitchen table, Jackson likely in his pajamas and Levi—well, no matter what he wore, he looked good. Suddenly I missed him terribly.

"Stop cheating the boy, mister," I said.

Jackson and I hadn't spent much time together until recently. Until Levi and I decided our relationship had moved past the let's-see-if-this-works stage. He was a great kid, and I was enjoying getting to know him. In fact, I had high hopes that he and Sydney would get along great since they were so close to the same age. Although both being only children, it could be dicey.

"Hey, Jackson," Levi said, "why don't we take a break. Go brush your teeth, and we'll finish up in a bit."

Without the slightest hesitation, I heard Jackson say, "K, Dad."

"K, Dad?" I repeated. "Did I hear that right? Because that was far too easy! No argument whatsoever? Is he for real?"

"He knows I'd beat him if he argued."

"Yeah, right," I said, chuckling. "There's a greater chance of a massive earthquake here in Minnesota."

"Don't let that get out. People think I'm tough. I have to uphold that reputation."

I chuckled. "Sure, tough guy."

"How was your girls' night out?"

"Super."

"Did you ladies solve the murder?"

"I have no idea what you're talking about, Mr. Wescott."

"Pshaw. Yeah, I'm sure you don't. Anything you want to share?"

"About what?" I asked.

"Remember I'm in this with you. Spill."

I thought about that a moment. "Truth." I let him in on what we'd discovered via social media sites. "Do we have a definite cause of death yet?"

"Nothing for certain. I mean poison, yeah, but what kind we won't know until the autopsy comes back."

"They can't even guess?"

"Babe, they're not going to let me in on that info. You know that. Besides, guesses aren't allowed in murder investigations. This isn't Clue. Lives aren't ruined if it's actually Colonel Mustard and you accuse Professor Plum."

"Can't you just kind of look around Walker's desk and—"

"No," he said. "I will not snoop."

"It wouldn't be snooping if you were looking for something else, would it? I mean—"

"No, Melanie. I am not going to screw this up. All that would do is hurt Claire."

"Only if you got caught. I could give you some pointers if you'd like. About not getting caught."

He made a sound as if he were trying not to laugh. "No."

"So, that means you won't do it?" I asked. His sigh let me know I was getting on his nerves. Just a tad.

"Oh!" I exclaimed after a brief pause. "I forgot to tell you I'm Rubie's date to Della's wedding evening after next."

"Should I be jealous?" he teased in a low voice.

"Very."

"I thought the evening after next is your Secret Santa reveal party with your staff."

"Oh!" I blurted, mentally problem solving on-the-fly. "I'll have to bump it back a day."

"You're going to inconvenience the rest of the ladies so you can snoop?"

"No. I'm moving it because Rubie wouldn't be able to be with us on Wednesday evening. And since she's doing the bride's hair, she can't very well not show at the wedding."

"Nice excuse." He chuckled.

"Fact. And Levi?" I said as I turned into my driveway.

"Yeah?"

"Stop cheating in the game you're playing with Jackson. Don't be a bully."

His deep laughter gave me a dose of warmth before I got out of my car to walk in the bitter cold to the house.

As soon as I reached my door, I saw a flash of headlights in my peripheral. I looked toward Claire's house to see her pulling into her garage. How did she make it home so quickly? She went to pick up Sydney from my grandmother's house after leaving Grizzley's. I shrugged it off and slipped into the house, heading straight for the thermostat. No fire in the fireplace tonight. It was getting late. I was tired yet too wired to sleep. Maybe I'd read for a while. I was halfway through an Agatha Christie novel. And, boy, could she write mysteries!

I finished taking off my coat, hat, and boots, placing everything in their proper places, then whipped out the napkin from my back pocket and transferred everything I'd written onto the whiteboard. I'd forgotten the piece of paper with more notes on my desk at the salon but jotted down some of the things I remembered, which was more than likely all of it.

I stood back and studied my additions. Tomorrow I would delve into checking up on Nick Frost to see if he knew who his replacement was. Just because Star Lane Santa Company didn't send anyone out, that doesn't mean Nick didn't plan the exchange with a friend. I would also see what I could find out about Norman and Trudy Flynn. Tourists densely populated Birch Haven in the summertime, but winters were far more intimate with only the locals.

Someone should know something about the two of them. Especially since they went to school here. However, most people who went to school in Birch Haven moved on after graduation.

I sighed and sat on the edge of my sofa, elbows on my knees, my chin resting on my folded hands. The only way Claire would have a good Christmas is if this were no longer hanging over her head. That gave me five days. God created the entire world in a mere seven. I had a glimmer of hope.

***

Tuesday morning, I woke to the news on my alarm announcing record low temps last night and this morning. In fact, it was so cold the temperature didn't even register on my outdoor/indoor thermometer display on my alarm clock. I shivered and shimmied back under my covers for a short minute before braving my feet on the cold floor, surprised to find it not as bad as I'd feared. Then I remembered I'd forgotten to turn the heat down before turning in last night. It was a surprise that I'd slept as well as I did.

I grabbed my thick black, red, and white fleece robe and tied the belt tight around me. After sliding into my slippers, I trotted downstairs to pour a cup of coffee and grab my devotional and iPad. I climbed back upstairs, snuggled into the reading chair in my bedroom, and tossed a Sherpa throw over my lap before settling in for my usual morning routine. I longed for summer mornings when I could perform my routine out on the balcony, more often than not at the same time that an orange sailboat sailed slowly and peacefully by on the lake. As soon as I would spot it, I continued watching it dreamily until it rounded the bend and out of sight. Someday, I'd told myself, I would go down to my dock and beckon him or her over to give me a ride. Or take up sailing myself.

I took a sip of coffee, said my prayers, and then grabbed my devotional book. This was one of the most enjoyable times in my day — quiet time for some self-reflection and maybe even a little self-improvement. My book fell open to a devotion on humility. *Ouch*! After reading the words, I took a few moments to ponder. *Humility is not thinking less of yourself, it's thinking of yourself less.*

I thought about the murder investigation. I was thinking about Claire, not myself, in this whole thing. *Wasn't I?* Or was I twisting the words to mean what I wanted them to. There was that darn guilt again.

Nana's words played in my head. *You are your own worst enemy, child.* I knew she was right. I expected nothing less than perfection from myself, and when I couldn't deliver, well…let's just say it's a good thing I don't expect from others what I expect from myself.

Lacking the peacefulness I usually get from this time, I set my devotional aside, opened the newspaper on my tablet, and skimmed through to see if there was any news on Patti's death. Nothing. That only told me that Walker hadn't solved it yet, and I had work to do. The minutes were ticking away. Hadn't Levi said the first 24 hours after a murder were the most critical? That finding the killer after that became increasingly more difficult? Twenty-four hours may be long gone, but I was going to make sure the killer wasn't.

I turned off my tablet, lay it on the side table, drained the last of my coffee, and headed for the shower. Working on things—anything—at the office put me in a different mindset and proved to be more productive. And that's what I needed to be right now— productive. I had five short days to deliver Claire's Christmas present to her: to clear her name in this case.

18

I pulled into the salon parking lot at seven o'clock and pulled up right next to the curb in front of the door to unload my car before moving it further out. Parking wasn't a problem, but we liked to keep the spaces nearest to the salon for customers. Sometimes, if we knew we would be leaving before dark, we even parked around the back. But only if it was broad daylight. And that never happened in the wintertime because daylight hours were few, and it was always dark by the time any of us left. It was a little creepy back there after dark.

I slid my whiteboard out from the back seat and hauled it and my purse in first. Next, I plugged in the tree lights before going back to my car to grab a couple of boxes of product I'd been storing in my basement. I dropped them on the front desk, then moved my car.

Coat, scarf, and mittens off and put away, I scurried to the coffee maker. First things first. We keep a small one-cup coffee maker in the office, but I had a lot of thinking to do, which required a lot of coffee.

As I scooped coffee into the filter, I paused, remembering the coffee was one of the possible causes of Patti's death. My cheeks flushed with shame. Claire was the one who served her the coffee. If I doubted the coffee, that meant I questioned Claire. And I didn't. I shook my head and finished the process, satisfied when the first gurgles sounded.

While I waited for it to brew enough liquid gold to pour into my cup, I scanned the day's appointments. Unless someone canceled, I had no open spots. I needed to work miracles this morning before the salon opened.

Finally, I was able to fill my cup from the still brewing coffee. I wrapped my hands around the warm mug and proceeded back to the office. I plopped in the chair behind the desk and studied my whiteboard. Nick Frost was going to be my starting point. I hoped he could tell me the name of the replacement Santa. And if it was typically the same cast of characters each year, he may have some information on Della and Howard. I felt a little bad that I'd never paid attention to who played what role before this, but I hadn't had any reason. I stayed in the salon and worked. If I trotted down to the grocery store at the other end of the mall to get my sweet treats and say hi to Stormi, I admired the decorations and lights, not who was behind them. Those of us without children don't have a reason to engage with those wearing the costumes. If I had a child, I might have made acquaintance with Mr. Local Santa. Sadness tugged at me.

I pulled out the notepad I'd tucked beneath the desk blotter and focused on the general vicinity Millie told me yesterday in which Nick lived. *Eastern outskirts of Birch Haven.* It didn't give me much to go on, but at least it was a start. I'd never frequented that side of town but how hard could it be?

I pressed the power button on my computer and waited a few seconds that felt more like minutes as it hummed to life. "You need a good strong cup of coffee, girl," I told it.

When the desktop background of Sydney popped up on the screen, I opened my search engine and typed in *Nick Frost, Birch Haven, MN*, then waited. Bummer. Not as easy as I'd thought. Up popped *images for nick frost, birch haven, MN* with several pine tree pictures to click on. Beneath that was *Nick Frost – Sales Specialist* followed by several items not remotely connected to what I'd hoped to see.

I tapped my pencil eraser on the desk. *Tap! Tap! Tap!* I thought of Claire, smiled, and tapped some more, willing my brain to think of an answer. I typed in *Nicholas Frost, Santa, MN*, resulting in several images of a rather grumpy looking Santa and several references to a movie with a picture of someone equally grumpy. I tried different variations for the spelling of Nicholas. Nothing useful popped up.

I sat back in my chair, tapping my pencil again, this time on the chair's arm, then sat back up and typed in *whitepages.com*, followed by the appropriate information in the proper boxes. Five Nick Frosts popped up but none in Birch Haven. Only one of them fit the age group I was looking for, however. I felt a glimmer of hope. This search would be worth paying the fee to get the extra information. I dug out my credit card and started the process.

After a half-hour of surfing the Net for anything else I could find on any of the other possible suspects—a search that yielded pretty much nothing except an address for Trudy—I bundled up and hiked on down to the grocery store for a blueberry cream cheese-filled croissant for me and a cherry Danish for Claire. While I was at it, I arranged for Stormi to hang onto the cupcakes for one more day since we had to push our Secret Santa reveal party back.

"Ew!" she said. "They'll have already been sitting in the cooler for a few days by the Wednesday date. And you want to let them sit one more?"

"So what's wrong with that?" I asked.

"A whole lot, that's what. I'll make you guys fresh ones."

"And waste the gems you've already made? You'll do no such thing," I argued. "I want the ones you baked for the contest. They are the cutest things ever." She gave me a sidelong look. "Seriously!" I insisted. "I want those."

She shrugged. "Fine. But don't tell anyone where they came from. I don't want people thinking I give out stale goods."

"Oh, for goodness sakes, Stormi!" I said, chuckling. "They're in the cooler. I've eaten things from the refrigerator that have been in there a lot longer than that."

"None of my stuff," she said.

"Gotta run. See you later." I turned to walk away before spinning around again. "Hey, do you know Nick Frost?"

She snickered. "Is that a joke? Don't you mean *Jack* Frost?"

"No. Nick Frost. That's the name of the guy that plays Santa."

"Was his mother clairvoyant or something?" Her eyes sparkled. Everyone seemed to have a comedic response to poor old Nick.

"So that's a no?" I asked.

She shook her head. "That'd be a no."

"What about Patti Parker?" I asked. "Or Trudy Flynn."

"Yeah, I know both of them. We all went to high school together. But I already told you that."

"What'd you think about Patti?" I asked.

"You seriously want to know? She was a terrible person in high school, and from what I've heard hadn't changed one iota."

"You never kept in touch with her?"

She scoffed. "Why would I? She isn't someone I would have ever chosen to be friends with."

"You and the rest of the town by the sounds of it," I mumbled. "What's your take on Trudy?"

Stormi laughed knowingly as if she had a secret I wanted in on. This story deserved my full attention, so I set my bakery bag down and listened.

"Patti and Trudy have hated each other since— well, since forever."

"Why?"

"There's some serious history between those two." A customer came up to the counter to look through the book of custom order cakes that lay open. "Help you?" Stormi asked, all business.

I waited while she helped the customer and gave her a pickup date and time. She came back to me. "Where were we?" she asked.

"Patti and Trudy's history."

She chuckled. "Ah, yes." She leaned against the display case, her arm resting on top. "Well, going waaay back," she said, "Patti dated this guy in high school—he's a guy I used to date before her—and Trudy took him from Patti." Stormi let out a hoot. "Being the one to have him first, let me tell you he was no prize. But you should have seen the hissy fit Patti threw. You'd have thought the entire world was coming to an end." Her eyes glittered with amusement at the memory. "Trudy ended up marrying him, which ticked off Patti even more. Make matters worse between them, I don't think Norman— that's the guy's name, Trudy's husband," she explained, "well, from what I've heard through the grapevine, I don't think he ever really got over Patti. And that just fueled the fire between those two even more."

"If Norman was so in love with Patti, why did he leave her for Trudy?"

She shrugged. "No one has ever been able to figure that out. It's not like she got pregnant or anything. We always thought she'd get knocked up, so when Della did—Della Lewis, the one I told you about—it shocked all of us. But this feud between Trudy and Patti went back long before that even. The whole Norman thing is just what made everything erupt like a volcano." She readjusted her red and white Santa hat and smoothed her black hair that hung below it.

I took a two-second trip down memory lane from my high school days and ended the journey quickly. I didn't have time for that. "Did Della Lewis marry the guy who—"

"Knocked her up? Yeah, but it didn't last long. Not even a year, if I remember right.

"That explains the last name difference."

"If it's even the same one," she said. "But I guess Della's not a common name."

"Did you know her brother?" I asked.

"Howard? Not very well. He was several years older than we were. In his senior year when we were freshmen."

"Hm. Yeah, same Della. There wouldn't be two of them from a small town, each with a brother named

Howard." I took a minute to process all that I'd learned. "I should have come to you earlier."

"What's this all about?" she asked. When I didn't answer right away, she narrowed her eyes and said, "Wait a minute. Are all of these people on your suspect list?" Again, I didn't answer. "Listen, Melanie, Trudy and Patti had their problems, but Trudy isn't a killer. And neither are Della or Norman. As I said, I didn't know Howard very well, but—well, if we're being honest, if one of them did, Patti probably had it coming."

"Stormi!" I said, my eyes wide.

"I'm just sayin'." She shook her head slowly and straightened her hat again. "That woman was evil and had more enemies than items I've baked."

"In most cases, when someone dies, you hear about all the good things they've done and what a wonderful person they were. No one likes to speak ill of the dead."

"Well," she said with a snort, "sadly, you won't see that here. Other than bumping into each other occasionally, I haven't seen Patti for years. But things don't appear to have changed much. Still a sourpuss, as far as I could tell."

"Huh," I said absently, thinking about what a sad life Patti must have had. I couldn't imagine going through life so miserable that I made everyone else miserable along with me. I snatched up the bag with my croissant and Claire's Danish. "I have to get going. Thanks for all the info."

"My pleasure. Should have asked me when you started your whole Sherlock thing. Could have saved you some time and brain cells."

"Truth," I said with a snicker. "See you later."

She waved a hand at me and stepped behind the counter to help another customer who'd begun flipping through the custom cake book.

***

By the time I got back to the salon, Claire was there, her orange SUV parked next to my car. I glanced at the time on my phone. Eight o'clock. Only an hour before we opened, but still early for her. She usually dropped Syd off at school for eight and came to work after that.

"Hello?" I called when I opened the door to an empty salon.

"Back here!" she called from the office.

I trotted back to see her sitting behind the desk, focusing hard on something. "What are you doing?"

"Keeping my mind busy by doing some of the bookwork."

I froze for a second. "You hate bookwork."

"*Thank you* would be a better response," she said.

Claire hated doing the bookwork, and I loved it, so it had always been an understanding between us that it was one of my responsibilities. I pressed my lips together, trying to keep from saying something, but I just couldn't. "Claire, really, you don't have to do that. Please," I added for good measure.

"It's better than sitting at home with nothing but time on my hands," she said, flipping me a smile that didn't quite reach her eyes.

"Yeah, but isn't there something else you'd rather do here? Something other than bookwork? Anything?" The desperation in my voice wasn't lost on either of us.

She pointed the pencil at me and narrowed her eyes. "Oh my gosh! You're afraid I'll mess something up."

My cheeks felt warm and I bit my lower lip. "I just have a system, is all."

Her jaw slackened, and her eyebrows drew close. "Melanie Hogan, you're a control freak, plain and simple."

"But you've always known that about me." I smiled coyly. Claire stared at me for a moment, and I thought about the time we had a small disagreement a couple of years ago. Ribbing that went too far, and how awful I felt afterward. I held my breath.

"Unbelievable," she finally said, shaking her head slowly. Her jaw slackened and her eyes softened.

I exhaled in relief. "Did you drop Syd off at school early?"

She gawked at me like I'd asked if she wanted to go swimming in the frozen lake. "It's Christmas break." Then she giggled. "Where's your head, girl?"

"Duh!" I rolled my eyes. "I've been so caught up in this," I poked my finger at the whiteboard, "that I can't even think straight."

"I'm not sure which of us is the bigger mess, you or me. Syd's still at your grandmother's house, anyway." I gave her a questioning look. "She called me when I was on my way to pick her up last evening and asked if she could spend the night. They were going to play Yahtzee."

"I've been replaced," I sulked, then grinned. "Nana and I used to play that all the time. I was wondering how you got home so fast last night." And then an idea hit me. "Nana!"

Claire gave me a sidelong glance. "What about her?"

"If Nick Frost has lived here for a long time, which it sounds like he has, I bet Nana would know him. Guess what I found out this morning?" I filled her in on the Birch Haven High School drama from years ago. When I finished, her mouth hung open, and she shook her head slowly.

"We didn't have that stuff happening when I was in high school back in Florida."

"Oh, it happened, Claire. It goes on in every high school. You just weren't part of it. And I'm not surprised."

"Were you?" she asked, wrinkling her nose.

I dropped my chin and stared at her. "What do you think?"

"No. You hate drama." She set the pen down and sat back, arms clasped behind her head. "So do you think Trudy hated Patti enough to kill her?"

"She's certainly at the top of my list," I said. "Wouldn't you agree?"

Claire nodded. "Did you tell any of this to Levi yet?"

I shook my head. "I guess I'm a little hesitant. I want to, and he wants to be involved, but I don't want him to get in trouble with the department for being *too* involved."

"And you think *you* won't get in trouble?" she asked incredulously.

"I can't lose my job over it, but he can. They can't do much to me except slap my hand. And that's only if Walker finds out. My plan is for that not to happen. Besides, I don't want to risk compromising the police investigation if Levi is involved in any way."

"Good thing I trust you and that you're good at this detective stuff. Otherwise, I'd be in deep trouble."

"They'll figure out soon enough that whatever poison it was that killed Patti wasn't in the coffee you served her."

"I sure hope so." She sighed and sat back in the chair.

I opened the white bag from the bakery. The smell of sugar and berries wafted out and my mouth watered. I set the cherry Danish in front of her, getting the smile I'd hoped for. "Do me a favor and let me get the coffee," I said, winking at her.

She grimaced. "That was a terrible joke, Mel."

I gave her a half-smile. "Yeah, I guess it was." A minute later I was back in the office and set her cup in front of her. "I'm going to call my grandmother and ask about Nick Frost."

"You do that. I'm going to feed my face." She pinched a piece of dough from the Danish and popped it in her mouth.

I picked up my phone and punched in the number assigned to Nana, my fingers crossed that she could fill in the empty blanks my earlier search had returned.

"Rose Donnelly's house," came a very grown-up sounding Sydney.

"Hey, girl. I heard you got to have a sleepover with my grandmother."

"Yup! We played Yahtzee until ten o'clock!" She sounded pretty pleased with herself. "Don't tell my mom."

"We're on the phone, kiddo. You don't have to whisper." Claire shot me an inquisitive look, and I waved my hand at her in dismissal, stood, and slipped out of the office and into the salon. I looked out the window as Rubie's car pulled up next to mine and Claire's. Babs and Connie would be arriving shortly. "Hey, can I talk to Gramma Rose?"

"Sure. Hold on."

The phone clunked in my ear as she set it down, and I winced. Seconds later, Nana's voice came on the line.

"Hello, dear."

"Hi, Nana. I have a question for you. Do you know a Nick Frost?"

"Santa? Doesn't everyone? One's never too old, you know," she said, amused.

"Very funny." I laughed gently and waved a hand at Rubie as she came through the door. I was grateful that she went back to the office instead of hanging out by me in the front.

Nana chuckled. "Why do you ask?"

"Do you? Know him."

"Just that he's the one who plays the Santa at the shelter every year for any kids there. He stops in before working the shindig at the mall where you work. Why?"

I've always been so proud of Nana for how involved she is in our town's homeless shelter. "Do you know if he showed? At the shelter, I mean."

"Why, no, he didn't. He'd never done that before, so Ada was worried about him." Ada was one of the shelter administrators. "Said in the past he called even if he would be five minutes late, dontcha know."

"Do you know where he lives?"

"I don't, but I can find out from Ada."

"Nana, that would be beyond fantastic!" I exclaimed. "Can you call her now?"

"What's the rush, dear?"

"It might be nothing. Can I fill you in this evening after work? I'll stop by."

"I'll call you back as soon as I get a hold of her."

"Thank you, Nana. You're the best!"

19

I was well into a hair color on my second client when my cell phone played the tune I had reserved only for Nana, "Wind Beneath My Wings." I excused myself from my client.

"I'll only be a minute," I said, placing a hand on her shoulder. "I've been waiting for this call." I hurried back to the office. "Hi, Nana. Whad'ya find out?"

"Ada didn't have an address but said he lives in that big white farmhouse on the East edge of town. The one with the wrap-around porch. You know the one I'm talking about?"

My heart started racing at the good news as I recalled the house. "I do! I'd always admired that place. It's about the only place I remember on that side of town."

"Granddad and I always loved it, too. Has gotten quite run down since his wife died, though. Used to have such beautiful flower beds all over. Now they're nothing but weeds if I remember right."

"Thank you so much, Nana! I have a client in my chair, so I have to run. But I'll be by sometime after work. Don't hold dinner for me, though. I'm planning on running out to Nick Frost's house to check if he's okay. He didn't show up for our festival either."

"Why that's so nice of you, dear," she crooned. "But what's the real reason?"

"What do you—"

"You wouldn't go to a strange man's house unless you had a reason. Will that man of yours be going with you?"

"Nick is hardly a strange man," I said, avoiding her question. "He's lived around here a long time. If Ada trusts him to come to the shelter and Star Lane Santa Company trusts him to be around children, I'd say it's safe. I'm sure they do background checks on their hires. Besides," I added, "wouldn't you feel better knowing he's okay?"

"Goodness gracious," she said, sounding like she'd resigned the situation. "Let me know what you find out."

"I will. And Nana?"

"Yes, dear?"

"Thank you. Love you!"

"Love you, too, dontcha know."

After sending my client out the door, I stared at the appointment book, wondering how soon I could finish my last client and get out the door before heading over to Nick's. I was deep in thought, planning my escape, when the ringing phone interrupted me.

"A Cut Above, this is Melanie."

"Oh, goodie! Just who I wanted to speak with. This is Mabel. I have an appointment with you late this afternoon."

I snickered. *Oh, goodie?* "Hi, Mabel. How can I help you?"

"Melanie, darling, I need to reschedule. And before Christmas. I know you're so terribly busy at this time of the year and trying to get in might be out of the question, but if there's any way—"

"Yes!" I interrupted. She'd just made my trip to Nick Frost's house easier. "I can get you in early tomorrow if you want. Before the salon opens."

"Oh, you're such a dear," she said. "You'd do that for me?"

"Of course. I'd be happy to. I'm here early anyway."

"Such a gem, you are. You take after that grandmother of yours."

I beamed. "Mabel, that's the biggest compliment you could give this girl."

"See you tomorrow," she said, sounding as happy as I was. "I'll be there at eight sharp."

"See you then," I said.

The appointment before Mabel's was a straightforward child's cut. If I hustled, I could be out of the salon and on my way to Nick's house by four-thirty. Before dark set in.

"Hey, Claire," I said as I cleaned up my station to prepare for my next client, a color. "Can you close today? My last client just rescheduled, and I have an errand I'd like to run before dark."

"Sure," she said readily. "Rubie and I both have sisters coming in for a cut and color, so we'll both be finishing up about the same time."

Claire and I are the only two with keys to the salon, and we avoid any of us closing alone after dark, which means one of us had to be here. "Perfect."

The rest of the day flew by in a flurry of activity. Babs turned out some pretty entertaining Christmas nail art, and between Christmas colors, a few perms on our blue hairs, and kids cuts, we hardly had time to scarf down lunch. Instead, we escaped to the office, taking bites here and there as time permitted. The laughter and salon chatter that I enjoy so much was lost on me all afternoon, however, as I wondered what I would find out from Nick when I got to his house. At first, I'd considered asking Rubie to go with me. That is until I found out she was closing with

Claire. It was more critical that we adhere to our salon policy. I hoped.

***

At four-twenty-five, I was in the car. I let it run for five minutes to warm up before heading to Nick's. Granddad always said driving with a cold engine was hard on the car. The sun was beginning to set, so I knew I had to hightail it if I would be there and gone before it completely disappeared.

I turned into Nick's drive and discovered last night's dusting of snow undisturbed except for a set of footprints and some critter tracks. But no tire tracks in sight. Maybe he was on vacation somewhere warm. Somehow, I didn't think so, though. The footprints in the driveway went toward the house, not from. I glanced toward his garage and his outbuildings. There didn't appear to be any sign of life anywhere. I shivered. "Get in and out of here fast, Melanie," I muttered.

I zipped my black leather coat up as high as it would go, tied my scarf around my neck, slipped my hat on my head, and shoved my hands into my mittens. I shut my door quietly behind me. Why, I didn't know. No one was around. My gut just told me it was the smart thing to do.

I peeked in the garage door window and saw a car parked there. Presumably Nick's. So he hadn't left town. Unless someone brought him to the airport. But if that was the case, the footprints were going the wrong way—if someone picked him up, the prints would be leading toward the road where a car might have pulled up. And why wouldn't he have called and canceled his Santa gig with the shelter and the mall?

The doorbell was busted, so I reached my hand up to rap my knuckles on the door but stopped before making contact. It was already ajar! My pulse picked up a notch, and I could see vapor materialize with each breath.

I looked all around me, then through the long, narrow window beside the door. I cupped my hands around my face and gasped when I saw an arm sticking out of what appeared to be a closet. I stumbled backward, catching myself on the old wooden railing. Before I could hightail it back to my car, I could have sworn I saw it move. I had to help!

I slipped through the door and ran to the closet. When I opened the door, a man who I assumed to be Nick Frost tumbled out, legs tied and mouth duct-taped. Rope circled one wrist, and there was a rope burn on the free wrist. He must have freed himself partway. I felt for a pulse. Weak as it was, at least there was one.

I froze when a floorboard creaked upstairs. I wasn't alone!

I snagged my phone from my back pocket and punched the number for Levi, my eyes darting around the room as I searched for a place to hide. What were the chances I could dash for my car and make it safely? Another creak sent me hurtling to the nearest open door, which turned out to be the bathroom. By the time this whole fiasco was over, I'd never use another restroom again.

Levi answered as I closed the door as quickly and quietly as I could. I cringed as the lock clicked, sounding loud in the quiet house.

"Wescott," he grumbled.

"Levi—"

"Melanie? Why are you whispering?" His tone did a 180 turn when he'd realized it was me calling.

I scanned the bathroom and shuddered. It was no secret that a man lived here alone. The filth might be a bigger threat than the kidnapper in the house.

"Melanie!" Levi said.

"I'm at Nick Frost's place. There's a man, I'm assuming Nick, in the closet, tied up and unconscious. He has a pulse but barely. There's someone upstairs." I hardly recognized my own voice. Or lack thereof.

"Good God! Get out of there now!" he commanded. "Someone will be right there." He barked orders to whoever was with him.

"I've locked myself in the bathroom."

"Melanie, you need to get out of there. Now!"

"I'll never make it to my car. Whoever is up there knows I'm here. I'd have to run past them."

Footsteps were now outside the bathroom door. My heart thumped when I realized I left my purse in the car, along with my concealed weapon. The one time it would be the most useful. All I had now were my keys, my phone, and whatever was in this room. I desperately searched the tiny room for a weapon of some sort. All I could find was a plunger.

I frantically focused on the small window above the toilet.

"Melanie, what are you doing? Why aren't you answering?"

I'd been so focused on escaping that I hadn't even heard Levi talking.

"I have to go," I whispered.

"No, wait!"

"There's a window here—"

The doorknob turned slowly, then stopped. In my scramble to open the window, I dropped my phone and heard a *kerplunk*! as it splashed in the nasty toilet bowl. *Gross*! My eyes darted between it and the window.

"Make this easy and just open the door," came a man's voice.

One more glance at my phone and I decided on the window. It was my only hope. I stood on the toilet seat, pushed the window open, and squeezed my body through the opening. I may be small, but the window was smaller, and my bulky coat didn't help. Good Lord! Why couldn't this have happened in the summer?

I got stuck halfway through but managed to wriggle free just as the door exploded open. I fell to the ground, thankfully landing in a snowbank.

I jumped up and surveyed the land around me. I was in the back of the house, and I had parked my car in front. I'd never make it there without getting caught. All hope of a fast, safe escape, much less of reaching my gun, vanished. There was a grove of trees and scrub brush not more than eight or ten yards in front of me. What lay on the other side, or how deep the forest was, I had no idea. But I knew if I could make it there, I had a chance of getting away.

I bolted toward the grove. Since arriving at the farmhouse, the light had suddenly gone out, almost like a candle. We were in the middle of the countryside, the nearest neighbors not visible through screens of trees. I couldn't even see lights from Christmas decorations. The only boon was the light from the full moon, bouncing off the white snow, making it feel more like four o'clock then five-thirty. I was grateful I could see where I was going, but that meant whoever came after me could see too. The ladies at the salon gave me a hard time for wearing black so often, but my black coat worked in my favor this time.

I glanced behind me as I ran, cursing my clumsiness at dropping my phone. I reached the edge of the trees, their bare branches looking like bony, arthritic fingers reaching for the sky. I didn't even have the benefit of leaves and foliage hiding me from view.

"You'll never get away!" the man said. "You'll freeze to death out there!"

Like he cared. Branches from shrubs bit my cheeks as I ran, shielding my face with my arms as best I could. I ran until my breath came in gasps, the cold pinching my lungs and nostrils. My face burned from places that got beat up by the branches. I slowed when I reached the edge of the wood and surveyed the area around me, trying to get my bearings. I was on Lumberjack Road. Not a well-traveled road but not completely untraveled, at least.

Sirens sounded in the distance, and red and white lights competed in the sky with the moonlight above the trees. Surely a car would come by soon. Maybe my chances were better if I made my way back to the house. If I didn't freeze to death before I got there. At least the police would be there before I was.

A branch snapped behind me, and I screamed. There stood a coyote watching me. I couldn't tell if it was hungry or wary. I struggled to remember what to do when meeting up with one, but my mind was as frozen as my body. All I could remember is not to run because it triggers their prey drive.

I stayed still as we stared at each other, he and I. My heart pounded in my ears. I tried to appear as big as I could and yelled, "Shoo! Shoo!" and waved my hands. My fingers were without feeling they were so cold. "Go away!"

I swear he smiled before he turned and walked away, completely disinterested, just as a car came around the bend. I exhaled my enormous relief. I would recognize that car anywhere, but I'd never been as thankful to see it as right now. It came to a screeching halt next to me. Levi!

20

Before Levi even stopped the car, I opened the door and jumped in, immediately placing my frozen hands in front of the heating vent. He pulled me toward him, and I melted into his body heat.

"Thank God you came when you did. I was almost dinner for a hungry coyote."

He squeezed a bit tighter. "If I weren't so happy to see you, I'd be mad right now. What were you thinking? Why didn't you call me to come out here with you? Why didn't you run for your car?"

"Because I was trapped in the biff." My voice sounded muffled against his neck. My lips were numb to the point where they couldn't pronounce the words appropriately. I hadn't realized how cold and numb I was until I'd begun warming up. "The only way out was the window, and that was on the backside of the house," I said. "My car was in front. There's no way I would have made it." I shivered and pulled back. "Did you see that wild animal eyeing me?"

"No."

"It was enormous!"

He chuckled gently and kissed the top of my head. "The big one that got away?" he asked.

"Hey, there, my friend, he would have eaten me up if you wouldn't have gotten here when you did. You saved my life."

"The person back at the house was far more dangerous to you than a little coyote. But all the same, I'm just glad you're okay." He pulled me toward him for another hug. "You scare the bejesus out of me, woman."

I pulled back again, stripped off my mittens, and held my hands back up against the heating vents. "How did you know where to find me?"

"Followed your tracks in the snow to the edge of the woods, and I knew where to go from there."

"Did they catch the guy?"

"It was a man?"

"Yup. Not a voice I recognized, though. Under the circumstances, I guess that's a good thing."

"Yeah, I guess you could say that. But if you did recognize him, it would certainly help the police."

"Where are you going?" I asked as he turned right off Lumberjack Road instead of left, which would have taken us back to the house. I grabbed the dash and turned to face him. "Nick's house is the other way."

"I'm taking you back to the salon."

"But my car is at the house."

"We'll get it later."

"Levi," I argued insistently, "I want to go back and get my car."

"You want to go back and get involved in whatever's going on out there."

I grumbled. "And I can't do that if you won't bring me there. And my purse is in my car. I need it!"

He glanced over at me and shook his head. "You almost got yourself killed, Melanie, and you want to go back for more?"

Lights from an oncoming car lit up his face. As my grandmother would say, *Uffda!* He wasn't a happy camper.

"Levi—" I struggled to think of the best argument to get back to the house. "Don't you have to be at the crime scene? I promise I'll get in my car and leave right away."

"Walker's handling it since you were involved once again. Geez, Melanie! At this rate, I'll never have another homicide to investigate." He shook his head again.

"He's dead?" I asked incredulously. "When I felt his wrist, there was a faint pulse."

"Sounded like he's hanging on but not by much."

"Will you keep me posted on his status?"

He studied me as if trying to decide how to answer. "Yes."

We turned onto the street where my salon was, and his phone rang. "Wescott." He listened intently then said, "Okay. Sure. Yeah, no, she's right here. Who's bringing her car?" Another pause. "Anderson? Okay." He parked up close to the salon entrance. Claire and Rubie's cars were still in the parking lot. "I'll be watching for him," he said into the phone. "As soon as he drops off her car, I'm taking her to St. Josephs to get checked out."

Before I could make a sound of protest, he held up a finger and narrowed his eyes. I exhaled and sunk back against the seat. The minute he hung up, I said, "I'm fine. I do not need to go to the hospital."

"You're getting checked out. You've got a couple of gashes on your face that need examining at the very least."

I instinctively touched my hand to my face and winced. "I know. And they hurt. But I'm not a child you can order around."

"No, but you are my girlfriend, who I happen to love. I want to be sure that there's going to be a wedding someday."

My breath caught. *Wedding*? "But—"

"Melanie, please."

His tone made me stop. If the shoe were on the other foot, I would want him checked out, too. I supposed now wasn't the time for me to forcefully insert my stubborn independence.

"Okay," I said. "But we're going to find out I'm perfectly fine." And then a thought occurred to me. "Are they bringing Nick Frost to St. Joseph's?"

"No, Melanie."

"They're not? Where will they bring him then? Considering he's still alive."

"I mean no, you're not getting any more involved in this than you already are. You're already neck deep in Patti's murder."

"What if they're connected?"

"We—as in the police—will figure that out."

"I thought you said you couldn't be involved in this one either. Will Walker know to look into—"

"Walker's a smart guy, babe. Trust him."

"Sure. It doesn't sound like Nick will be able to talk anyway," I quipped. "I just want to be sure he's okay is all. But you promised to let me in on status updates if you get them." He didn't say anything. "Right?"

"Yes." But it didn't sound too convincing.

I opened the car door before he came around to open it for me, something he did unless I beat him to it. It was still something I had a hard time getting used to.

Claire and Rubie were standing behind the desk, talking. Both gawked at me, and their eyes grew huge.

"What happened to you?" Claire gasped.

"Oh, my gosh, Mel!" Rubie exclaimed. "What'd you go getting yourself into this time?"

Levi tossed her a knowing look and then turned toward me. "Yeah, Blondie, what you get yourself into this time?"

Rubie plucked dried twigs from my hair, and Claire grabbed a towel and began dabbing my cheek and forehead. I felt like a baby tiger being groomed. I pulled back from them.

"Stop moving," Claire scolded, pulling me toward her by my arm. "You're bleeding. A lot."

"I'll be fine," I insisted.

"What happened?" she asked.

"I might have stumbled upon an almost dead Nick Frost," I said reluctantly.

"*Might* have?" Claire asked, her voice rising an octave.

I shrugged a shoulder. "Okay, I did."

"Levi," Rubie said, her hand resting on my shoulder, "what happened?"

"Why are you asking Levi?" I asked. "He wasn't there. I was." As briefly as I could, I filled them in on the past couple of hours. "And you wouldn't have believed the gigantic coyote that almost ate me right when Levi pulled up."

"Yeah," Levi said and smirked. "I didn't see said coyote."

"Wipe that amused look off your face, buster," I scolded. "He was there. And I would have been his dinner had you not shown up when you did."

"Melanie, you get yourself into the worst predicaments," Claire said, wrapping an arm around my shoulders and pulling me toward her, blotting at my face again. "Had I known that was the so-called errand you had to run, I would have refused to close up the shop. What were you thinking going there alone?"

"That's exactly what I asked her," Levi said.

"Are you okay?" Rubie asked. "I mean, shouldn't she get checked out by a doctor?" She asked Levi.

"Officer Anderson is bringing her car. He should be here any minute. And then I'm taking her to St. Joseph's."

"I can drive myself if you have someplace else to go," I said.

"Right!" All three said unanimously.

"Like you would go," Rubie said.

"We would have to follow you just to be sure," Claire added.

Levi gave me an "I-told-you-so" look. I rolled my eyes. "You're all impossible," I grumbled, then eyeballed Levi. "How did Anderson get my keys?"

"You gave one to me, don't you remember?"

"So you just give it out to anyone?"

"Anderson is hardly anyone. And why are you so obstinate? You're the one who nosed where you shouldn't have."

"I'd like to remind you that I'm the one who almost got eaten by a mammoth coyote."

Levi chuckled. "Come 'ere, babe," he said, holding out his hand to me. I glared and stayed rooted in place until I couldn't resist the pull. "I'm sure glad that coyote didn't get you," he whispered into my hair as he wrapped his arm around my waist. "I would miss your orneriness."

I knocked my hip against his. "I'm going to head to the loo to clean up a bit. I'll be right back."

Rubie snickered. "I think you should stay away from the loo from here on out."

I made a face at her and grimaced at a slice of pain before exiting the room.

The second the door closed behind me, I leaned back against it, exhaled long and slow, dropped my chin to my chest, and closed my eyes. My cheek and forehead throbbed. I gently pinched the bridge of my nose and rubbed my eyes with my thumb and forefinger. Upon gathering my wits about me, I opened my eyes, pushed myself away from the door, and reached on the top of the shelving unit for a fresh box of tissues, losing my balance as I did. I grabbed the corner post, dragging the unit a few inches, the bottom scraping on the floor.

"You okay in there?" Rubie hollered, her shoes clicking on the floor and now standing right outside the bathroom door.

"Never better," I hollered back.

"Let me in," she said.

"No. I'm fine, Rubie. Promise," I said through the door. "Just knocked the shelf is all." I listened for her steps to retreat.

I leaned my shoulder into the shelving unit to push it back into place, and as I did, I spotted the corner of a piece of paper peeking from beneath the back of the unit against the wall. I squatted down and used my pointer finger to draw it out.

When it was fully in view, I noticed it was torn in half, but there was enough to see that it was part of a cheaply printed certificate for a baking contest in which Patti had won first place. *What*? I'd never have pictured Patti as the baking kind. Or having anything to do with a kitchen. I imagined her ordering servants but not doing anything that required getting dirty.

It appeared there was more to Patti than met the eye. But on the back of the certificate was an even bigger surprise—a scribbled note that was somewhat illegible, including the author's initials. Unfortunately, the initials weren't readable and could be interpreted in several ways. But given the content of the note, Patti had been involved where she shouldn't have been. A motive for murder became clear. Now I just needed to figure out who.

"Mel?" Claire's voice with a knock on the door. "You okay?"

"Be right there," I said, folding the paper and tucking it in my back pocket. I splashed cold water on my face and winced as it touched the cuts and scrapes. I grabbed a paper towel and stood, studying my battle wounds in the mirror. "Meh," I mumbled, barely audible. "Nothing a little makeup and creative hairstyling can't conceal."

I finished blotting my face dry and strode back to the front, pointing out the window as I did. "My chariot is here." Anderson pulled up behind Levi's car in front of the salon entrance, and another car pulled in behind him. "What is this, a parade?"

"Someone needed to follow Anderson to get him back to his car."

I elbowed him gently. "Maybe you should go out there and see what the latest is at the crime scene."

"I'll do that," he said, giving me a gentle smile.

Claire and Rubie stood one on either side of me as I tried to read Levi and Anderson's lips. Neither of the ladies talked, probably realizing it wouldn't do any good. And probably realizing that I'd been through enough without more scolding. Claire can't scold anyway. It always came across as a loving tone. Counterproductive. And Rubie—well, Rubie could give as well as I could. But even she apparently decided I'd had enough for the evening.

Five minutes later, Levi clapped Anderson's arm and came back inside the salon.

"Come on, Blondie. Let's go get you checked out."

"Honestly, I'm fine. I would have died by now if something had been wrong," I said.

"Stop pouting," he said. Amusement danced in his eyes. "Come on. We'll come back and get your car when we're done."

21

We rode in silence to St. Joseph's. There was nothing left to be said right now, yet a lot to think about. The light from the moon made it difficult to see the stars. What a shame, because it was a clear sky tonight. Part of why it was so cold. Granddad always said it's coldest if the skies are clear, and I believed him. This evening was proof.

"What are you thinking about?" Levi's voice broke into my thoughts of Granddad as we pulled into a parking space.

I opened my door and got out, wrapping my scarf around my neck. "Nick is about the same age as my Granddad was when he died. He's probably someone's father and some kid's grandfather." I shrugged. "I just hope he's okay." And then felt the need to add, "And no, not so I can talk with him. Although, that would help." I mumbled the last sentence quietly, immediately feeling guilty.

Levi shook his head slowly and rested an arm across my shoulders. "Come on, my love. While you're getting checked out, I'll go see what I can find."

"You will?" I asked. I was a little surprised and wondered what the catch was. "And you'll let me know whatever information you get?"

He chuckled. "Yes, I'll let you know. Why is that hard for you to believe? I thought we agreed I was going to help you. After all," he looked down at me and wiggled his eyebrows, "I get a trip with you all to myself after this is over."

I giggled, wincing when pain sliced through my cheek. "No reason."

"Uh-huh," he said as he stepped to the side, allowing me to go first through the automatic door.

"I'm telling you I'm okay, Levi. Other than my face, nothing is wrong. I feel silly."

"We're doing this for me."

"Well, in that case…"

We stepped up to the front counter. It came up to my chest, but he towered over it. I checked in, and Levi interjected when I made light of the situation.

As soon as the receptionist pushed paperwork across the counter to fill out, I said to Levi, "Why don't you go check in on the *real* patient." He didn't move. I exhaled and shook my head. "Don't worry. I won't jet out of here." He studied me for a moment. "Promise," I said.

He stood up. "I'll be back in a jiff."

I watched as he headed south, then quietly got up and peeked around the corner as he pressed the elevator button for the sixth floor—Intensive Care. I swallowed a chuckle. He really thought I'd buy that? Nick hadn't been in the hospital long enough to go anywhere outside of the Emergency Room. I shook my head and sat back down.

Surprisingly, I was called back to a room within five minutes of turning in my paperwork, unheard of in the ER. Especially since three other people were waiting.

The doctor, on the other hand, took a while—as in a long while—to come into my room. I took advantage of my wait and wandered around the hall. When a nurse asked if she could help me, I claimed I had to use the restroom.

"Can't help me there," I said, grinning.

She gave me an odd look and left me on my way. As soon as she left, I passed the ladies' room, rounded the corner, and stayed close to the wall. I crossed my arms in front of me, tucking the one with the admissions wrist band behind my other arm.

Peeking around another corner, I stopped short. Levi was talking with an officer in the hallway. Just as I suspected. Apparently he thought I had a head injury and was unable to think clearly. *Men*!

I watched for a few minutes and jumped when someone touched my arm.

"Melanie Hogan?" a nurse asked. She picked up my arm and glimpsed at the wristband. *Darn it*! I'd let my guard down and uncrossed my arms at the wrong time.

"Yes."

"You need to stay in your room, ma'am."

My face flushed. "Of course," I said. I did an about-face and followed her back to my room like an obedient child.

***

After I was cleared, I went back to the waiting room to find Levi slumped in a chair and reading a magazine as if he'd been there for hours.

"Been waiting long?" I asked him.

"Nope. Everything good?"

"Everything's good," I assured him. "Just as I suspected."

"Looks like your battle scars were a bit worse than you thought," he said gently.

A laceration on my cheek next to my nose and one on my forehead required Dermabond. "Superglue fixes literally everything. What'd you find out?"

"About Nick?"

"No. About the cost of wireless service in the Bahamas."

He raised his eyebrows. "Fantastic! That's where you want to go for our getaway? I'm in!"

"Levi," I warned as I scowled and elbowed him. Though I was looking forward to time away together more than I had expected, I wasn't one to stray far from my home. Not even if it was the Bahamas.

"He's in critical condition but hanging in there. Unconscious, so they haven't been able to talk with him yet."

"So, what room is he in?" I asked innocently.

"I didn't pay attention."

"Yeah?" We were almost to the car. "What floor?"

"Sixth."

I gasped. "Liar!" He exhaled, groaned, and dropped his head back. "You honestly didn't think I would figure it out? You purposely tried to deceive me." I tried to sound angry but was pathetically unsuccessful.

"I'm only trying to keep you safe."

He opened my door for me, and I narrowed my eyes at him before sitting down. "By lying?" I shook my head and chuckled. "I can keep myself safe."

"Like tonight?" He closed my door, went around to his side of the car, sat down, and turned on the engine. He blasted the heater, then turned toward me. His eyes looked deep into mine. "This could have had a very different and unfortunate outcome, Melanie."

"I know. The world's largest coyote could have eaten me."

He smiled. "That sucker just keeps getting bigger and bigger. But how about we get serious for a minute here. Please?"

I turned my attention out my window then back at him. I stayed silent. I knew how close I'd come to death tonight. And not from the coyote.

"In my defense, Levi," I said, my voice nearly drowned out by the fan from the heater, "how was I to know that someone crammed Nick in a closet like a stuffed animal and a potential killer was in the house? I mean, come on."

He nodded and took my hand in his. "I agree, you couldn't have. But—"

"I knew there would be a *but* involved," I said, rolling my eyes.

"You went there hoping to get answers to Patti's murder. You had to have known there could potentially be something sinister."

He had me there. "I guess I didn't think it through very well." It was unnerving how often that was happening with this case.

"Admitting the problem is the first step." His eyes smiled.

"I thought you wanted seriousness."

He winked at me. "Come here." He pulled me toward him and wrapped me in a hug. "You're going to kill me one of these days. If anything ever happened to you—"

"It won't." My voice was muffled against his coat. "Unless you don't let me go, because I can't breathe."

"Let's go get your car. I'll follow you home."

"No need. I'll be fine."

"But what if—"

"No," I insisted. "You can't spend your time babysitting me. Go, do your thing. Keep your antennae up for any change in Nick's condition and keep me posted."

"Fine. But I'm calling every half hour to check on you."

My jaw dropped open in feigned outrage. "How's a girl supposed to get some sleep with that going on?"

"Like you're going to sleep," he guffawed. "I know you. You'll be back at that whiteboard of yours."

I lifted my hands, palms up, and shrugged.

Levi waited while I let my car heat up for a few minutes. As I turned onto the road from the parking lot, he turned the opposite way toward the precinct.

The green LED numbers on my dashboard rolled to seven-fifteen. Since my phone took a dive into the toilet, I'd called my grandmother from the hospital phone and let her know I ran into a bit of a roadblock, not to hold dinner for me, and I would be there as soon as possible. When she asked me what type of roadblock, I fibbed a little. *Helping a friend*, I'd said. It was enough to stop any more questions for the time being.

When I pulled into her driveway, the light above the kitchen sink shone above the biscuit-colored café style curtains. The living room drapes were pulled tightly together, not so much as a sliver of light shining through. As much as I loved visiting Nana, tonight I just wanted to be home and not have to field any questions. If I could convince her not to heat anything for dinner, I'd be good to go after fifteen minutes or so. And then I remembered my face stuck together with Dermabond. A quick visit without questions was not to be.

***

The following morning brought with it aching muscles and skin pulling against the facial superglue. I touched the wounds and whimpered as I reached for my phone. It wasn't there. "What the—" And then I remembered my phone in the toilet at Nick's house.

I groaned as I sat up and swung my feet around to touch the floor. My first stop of the day had to be the phone store. Thank the good Lord I insisted on taking out insurance on my phones. Rubie teased me that I was crazy for paying that much extra for as careful as I tended to be. Little did either of us know then.

I turned on the bathroom light and squinted against the brightness. I sure liked waking up to natural light coming through my skylight in the summertime rather than this harsh artificial stuff. Darkness held far more real estate in Minnesota during the winter months. And yet I loved it here and couldn't imagine living anywhere else except maybe on a beach in Mexico with nary a care. *Nah,* I thought, *not even there.*

I caught my reflection in the mirror and groaned yet again. Dark circles under my eyes revealed my lack of sleep even though I'd gotten home at a reasonably early hour. Once Nana digested the condensed version of events on which I'd filled her in and let her know how exhausted I was, she packed up dinner in Tupperware containers and sent me on my way. As soon as I got home, the Tupperware containers went into the refrigerator unopened. Except for the chocolate peanut butter pie. That one went straight to the dishwasher after I licked it nearly clean.

Distracted by the coffee maker's glorious sounds downstairs, I went to my nightstand to reach for my phone. Again. *Geez!* How many times was I going to reach for it? I missed it like crazy. Enough to give Levi a run for his money, that's for sure.

Even before pouring a cup of coffee, I jumped in the shower. I'd pour my coffee to go if time ran out. If I could get to the phone store as soon as they opened, I could be in and out in half an hour without having to take a number and wait to be called.

When I pulled up, there were already eight cars in the parking lot. I guess I wasn't the only one with the genius idea of getting here early. Several people huddled in front of the building, but I waited in my warm car until I saw a gentleman unlock the door and hold it open for the gang.

As soon as I went in, I searched the phone displays, found the one closest to the one I had, and brought it up to the counter.

"Did someone help you?" the employee behind the counter asked.

"Excuse me?"

"Did someone help you with the phone? We work on commission."

"Oh," I said and shook my head. "No. I knew the exact one I wanted."

"Do you have your old phone?" he asked, looking at me expectantly.

"Um—no, I don't. It kind of took a swim in the—well, let's just say cell phones may be water-resistant, but they aren't waterproof." I thought of my phone in the filthy toilet and shuddered again.

A man standing next to me chimed in and said, "No, they're not. I've had to replace my son's phone three times for that exact reason. And he's only sixteen." He shook his head. "Thank God for insurance." He was tall and had a pouch of a stomach straining the zipper on his parka.

"Right?" I said, feeling odd justification from this stranger. A woman bundled up like she lived in north-central Siberia sidled up on the other side of him, and he turned his attention to her. The two started discussing something between them.

"I can get my stuff from the Cloud, right?" I asked the sales attendant.

"Sure can!"

I restrained myself from jumping over the counter and planting a big kiss on the guy. "I'm technologically challenged. How hard is it?"

"I can send you off with instructions and a support line to call for assistance. Your carrier has one of the best helplines."

"At least there's that," I mumbled. I was beyond thrilled that I hadn't lost all of my data. *It's the small things in life, Melanie,* my grandmother likes to tell me. She's right.

When I turned to leave, I said to the man next to me, "You folks have a good day."

"Yes, you, too," he said. The woman was already scoping out the phone cases with all the bling. I admired my plain black case and tucked it in my purse. To each his own.

22

Despite starting at eight that morning to fit in my reschedule from yesterday afternoon, the day at the salon cruised by at lightning speed. Rubie and I both looked forward to Della's wedding that evening, both for very different reasons. Rubie for the social aspect as well as the food, cake, and dancing. Me because I wanted some answers. But I had to admit, the cake did hold a certain appeal.

Della had invited both of us to stay for the wedding and the reception afterward in lieu of payment. Odd, I thought. But Rubie was elated, and who was I to argue? More time to snoop around. Besides, the payoff had the potential to be better than cold, hard cash. And Levi couldn't possibly be worried about me hunting for information there. After all, what could go wrong at a wedding in a room full of people? But as soon as that thought crossed my mind, an uncomfortable feeling settled in the pit of my stomach. Because I knew the answer to that: *Plenty!*

That day Claire more than asked me to stop looking into the murder; she begged me. "I've been giving this a lot of thought," she'd said. "We need to trust the police, Mel. Trust in the department that Cole and Levi work for."

"If they were on the case I would," I'd argued. "I don't know about this Walker dude. If we can trust him."

"Cole said he's good."

"So did Levi. But still."

"Trust the process," she'd said, an echo of Levi's words. "Trust that the justice system works."

I almost choked on the drink of coffee I'd just taken. "Sure," I'd told her. "You do know it's called the *Criminal* Justice System, right?"

At that, Claire had just smiled, shook her head slowly, and given up.

Christmas was in three days. A spark of anxiety churned in my chest at the limited time I had.

Rubie bolted out the door after her last client left at five-o-five. The wedding was at seven, and she had to be at the church by five-thirty. I told her I would meet her there as soon as I was done, no later than six, in case any of the bridesmaids needed help with their hair or makeup. And as soon as my last client left at five-forty-five, I ran into the office, changed into the appropriate wedding attire I'd brought with me that morning, and was out the door in record time.

When I pulled into the church's small parking lot, I spotted Rubie's car and pulled up next to it. I grabbed my supplies bag from the back seat and headed toward the church. A woman in a lavender bridesmaid dress opened the door.

"You're Melanie? Thank God you're here," she said without giving me time to answer. "None of us had time to line up someone to do our hair since Della moved up the wedding so quickly. We're all trying to do our own, but it's pathetic. Absolutely pathetic." Her eyes were glassy from unshed panic tears.

Rubie stood behind her. "Melanie, this is Cindy. She needs an updo."

"On it," I said. "Lead the way."

They turned down a hallway, and I followed. "Silver's good," Rubie said, gesturing toward her. "She braided her own hair."

"Other than me," Cindy said, "it's just Kiki and Brandi."

"I'll be done with Della's hair in just a few minutes, so I can get Brandi if you can get Kiki and Cindy," Rubi said.

"Of course." Where did these people all meet, College of Odd Name Design? Della, Silver, Kiki, Brandi — sounded more in line with a strip club.

I glanced around the room, taking in the situation. My eyes hurt from all the lavender chiffon. At least it wasn't tulle. I detested anything made of tulle, even if it was black. But lavender? *Ugh!*

I set my bag down on a table, opened it, and started taking out supplies. "Okay, who's first, Cindy or Kiki?" I struggled not to snicker when I said the name *Kiki*.

"Me," Cindy said. "I need time to get my daughter ready. She's the flower girl," she added with evident pride. I glanced around the room. "She's with her dad in the lobby," she said as if reading my mind. "I told him I would be out to get her once I'm ready."

I looked over at Kiki, who was tipping back a flask. I could see from just a glance that if she didn't ease up, she'd soon be tipping over with it.

"Kiki, knock that off," the bride scolded. "At least wait until after the ceremony."

"Well, if you hadn't stopped —"

"Stop indeed," Della quickly interrupted.

"Stop what?" I asked.

"Nothing," Della answered. "She's had a bit too much already." She frowned at Kiki as Rubie stilled her head to continue working on her hair.

I turned up the radio a bit. I needed to talk to Cindy without anyone else hearing. "Anyone mind?" I asked. "I work faster to music."

"Heck, no!" Kiki answered, pumping her fist in the air. "It's party time, ladies!" Della scowled at her. Rubie turned her head back again.

Cindy sat down on a stool, and I began to work. I stuck a few bobby pins between my lips and started pinning as I went along.

"So you and Della go back a ways?" I asked around the pins.

"We used to work together," Cindy said. "Until she up and quit to move across the country with Donny. That's her husband-to-be," she explained.

"You must know each other pretty well."

"Oh, yeah."

I waited for her to stop nodding before I continued. "What kind of work do you do?"

"Sales."

I waited for more, but she said nothing further. "What kind of sales?"

"Pharmaceutical."

I struggled to maintain expressionless. "Yeah? That must be interesting."

"Meh," she said, screwing up her lips. "It pays the bills. But you must love your job, huh? I mean, how much fun would it be to do hair every day?"

Clearly, talk about Della was over. But all hope wasn't lost. Booze makes for loose lips, and Kiki was up next. I glanced over as she tipped back the flask again. It was almost empty.

Rubie finished up with Della as I began working on Kiki's frizzy brown hair. I started applying some product, taming the frizz.

"Girl," Della told her, "you need to stop coloring this mop before it all falls out."

"You kidding?" Kiki squealed. "I've already gone gray. I'm thirty-five and gray already! That's so not fair!"

Della and Silver began talking, and it wasn't long before they were deep in private conversation. At one point, each glanced at Kiki and me, neither looking comfortable. Della headed for the radio.

"Hey, ladies," she said, "I'm going to turn this down a bit so we can hear each other talk and ourselves think."

Darn! Just when I had an opportunity to get some useful info from Kiki.

"So, how do you and Della know each other?" I asked Kiki, striving to keep my voice beneath the music.

"Our kids know each other."

"Your kids?" I blurted.

"Yeah. They've been best buds since kindergarten. Mine's not here, which means I get to drink a little and enjoy myself." She grinned.

A little? I'd be interested to see how she has more than a *little* fun. "Where's Della's kid?" I asked, looking around as I pinned a piece of hair.

"Not here. She refused to come. Her and Della are going through some stuff. Jenny's not moving with Della and Donny. She's staying here with her dad."

A spark of recognition crossed my mind. And then I remembered. "Jenny?"

"Yeah. Della's kid."

"I might have seen her at the Birch Haven Christmas Festival." I explained what I remembered about Jenny, which was pretty much every detail.

Kiki grinned. "Yup, that's her!"

Della's head snapped around to look in our direction at Kiki's statement, which was louder than the music.

I thought about Kiki's words. Hadn't Toni said Jenny's mom wasn't at the festival? Poor kid was probably embarrassed that her mom was dressed as an elf and didn't want anyone to know.

"Do you know Della's brother very well?"

"Howard?" Kiki's eyes turned dreamy. "That man is so hot! What I wouldn't give for—"

"Kiki," Della said, now standing right by her side, "what kind of babble are you telling Melanie?"

"Talking about Howard," Kiki said. "When are you going to set us up?"

"I'm not," Della said.

Kiki placed her hand beside her mouth as if telling me a secret. "She's as protective of him as he is of her."

"Yeah?" I said. "And how protective is that?" Della wasn't amused with Kiki in the least. Nor me at the moment.

"Enough to not set him up with someone who can't stay sober long enough to stand up for me at my wedding."

I spun Kiki's stool so she faced sideways and looked at Della. "Must be nice to have a brother to protect you. I don't have any siblings."

She smiled, genuine affection reflecting in her eyes. "Yeah, he's gotten me out of a scrape or two."

"Such as?" I prodded.

She shrugged a shoulder. "Just stuff." She bustled away, conversation over.

Man! Maybe after her vows she would have a drink or two and start talking a bit more.

***

Rubie wanted to attend the ceremony, but I wasn't interested in the slightest bit. I encouraged her to go while I hung back and waited. Honestly, the wedding freaked me out a little since Levi had just mentioned it. I needed some time to adjust to that thought. In the end, Rubie pulled a couple of vodka shooters from her purse and decided to hang back with me.

As soon as the song, "Signed, Sealed, Delivered," by Stevie Wonder began playing, indicating the ceremony was over, we jumped up and followed the crowd next door to the event hall. The women shivered, arms crossed in front of them, as they ran in heels down a partially cleared sidewalk. I held my breath, waiting for one of them to slip on a patch of ice and break a bone. I trailed in at the end after the last one entered the hall.

The staff busily finished last-minute touches on the snack table. Most of the people were already at the bar or quickly headed there. Rubie and I stood to one side, watching. She was more interested in what everyone was wearing. Me—well, I paid not the slightest attention to that. I was too busy watching who talked to whom, reading body language, and trying to recognize faces.

Mostly I watched Della and Howard. Della's glass seemed to remain full, but I never saw her make a trip to the bar. And I never saw her take a drink. Bummer. Howard, on the other hand, made several trips to the bar.

On one of those trips, I sauntered up, accidentally bumping into him.

"Oh!" I exclaimed. "I'm so sorry!" I snatched a napkin from the bar and began dabbing at the lapel on his tuxedo.

"Hey, not a problem," he said, blatantly leering at me. When his gaze lingered a little too long, I shivered. Creep! "Can I get you a drink?" he asked.

I swallowed my displeasure with this guy. "Seems I should be fetching you one since I just spilled yours. What are you drinking?"

"Club soda."

His answer flustered me. "Club soda?" I managed to repeat.

"Why so surprised?" He grinned.

"I—I'm not," I blubbered.

He laughed. "It's okay. I used to imbibe too much, but no more. All this is natural. No more unhealthy substances go in this body."

He held his arms out at his sides as if inviting me to look. *No, thank you.*

"So you're Howard," I said.

"Thank you for the reminder."

Had I not considered him a possible murderer—and if he wasn't flirting so blatantly—his amusement might not have irritated me as much as it was.

"I'm Melanie," I said, holding out my hand. "I did the bridesmaids' hair. The ladies were talking, and rumor has it you're extremely protective of your little sister."

He shook my hand. "Yeah, my sister hasn't always made the best life choices. I've had to bail her out a time or two." He raised an eyebrow and cocked his head to one side. "Or three or four. But she's finally pulled it together. That's how she got Donny. He's a good guy, ya know? I'm not going to let anything ruin that."

"Like what?"

The lights went down, and a slow song started to play. He winked at me. "Wanna dance?"

I glanced at my watch. "Oh, man! Look at the time! I need to get home to my kids."

"Kids?" he asked, surprised.

"Yeah." I smiled sheepishly. "I have seven of them. All under six! It's pretty crazy at my house. But maybe we can hang out sometime. You know, with the kids."

Howard's jaw dropped. "Uhh, yeah. I'm a pretty busy guy. But, hey, you have a good night, Melanie."

And just like that, he was gone. Vanished. As in completely disappeared. I scanned the area and then hurried to the other side of the dance floor where Della and Rubie stood talking around a high-top table. I slid up beside Rubie.

"Hey, ladies!"

"Where have you been?" Rubie asked. "I was looking for you to head out."

"I caught her just in time. Trying to get to everyone is exhausting," Della said, looking every bit exactly that. "But I especially wanted to get to the both of you to thank you for saving the day with such short notice."

"It was our pleasure," Rubie said, giving her a slight side hug.

"I was by the bar talking to Howard," I said as I watched Della.

"He hit on you?" she asked with a chuckle.

"No," I lied.

"He didn't?" Her jaw dropped. "He must be coming down with something! Kiki would do anything to get him to notice her, but he doesn't have the slightest interest." She snickered and shook her head. "He'll be single forever. He's one of those bad boys who the ladies love, and he only loves the thrill of the chase."

I almost gagged. "He told me he got you out of some scrapes in the past. How lucky you are to have someone like that!"

"Yeah. My real knight in shining armor. Most girls I know don't have that," she said. Her voice filled with emotion. "My dad told him to let me fall on my face for once, but Howard wouldn't hear of it."

"What kind of trouble did he get you out of?" I asked.

She paused briefly then shrugged before saying, "I guess it's safe now. The vows are done, the ring is on." She held her hand up and admired her bling. "Let's just say I took advantage of my job. Or rather the ease with which I could get supplies. But I'm a changed woman now."

"Pharmaceutical supplies?" I asked. "Like Oxy?"

"Melanie!" Rubie scolded, eyes narrowed.

Della touched Rubie's arm. "It's okay, Rubie. It's all in the past. Besides," she held up her hand, admiring her ring again, "like I said, I'm hitched now. I don't have to worry about Donny dumping me." She looked at me. "I sold some pills on the side. And, yes, Oxy. You'd be amazed at how easy it was to get them and even easier to sell them. They're in pretty high demand."

The lightbulb in my head lit up. "That's why you ran from the police the day of the festival," I said.

"Well, yeah. Why else would they have been there? I mean I don't do it anymore, but I wasn't taking a chance and risk getting married in a jail cell. Or not at all." She looked adoringly at her husband who was engaging in horseplay with two of his groomsmen across the dancefloor.

"Was Patti one of your customers?" I asked.

Della's surprise was palpable, and she blanched. "Yes. But I told her I wasn't going to be her supplier anymore. I've stopped."

"How did she take that news?"

"Not well, I'm afraid." She smiled bitterly. "She threatened to rat me out."

"Bet that made you mad." I winced as Rubie's heel squarely connected with the top of my foot.

"I wouldn't say mad," Della said, "but it certainly concerned me. Donny doesn't know about my side-hustle. Things were finally going good for me, ya know?"

"I can't imagine it hurt your feelings to have the threat eliminated rather than to risk Donny finding out."

"Melanie," Rubie grumbled under her breath.

Della gave me a sidelong look. "Listen, I did not kill Patti Parker. I pushed pills, but I'm not a killer."

"With Howard so protective, would he have made sure Donny never found out?"

In a flash Rubie's hand was on my bicep, yanking me away from the table. I stole a glance over my shoulder as Della threaded her way through a maze of people on the dancefloor toward her beloved husband.

23

I slept well that night for a change. Except for my foot aching from Rubie stomping on it. I was sure to have a good bruise from that. She'd read me the riot act as soon as we left the wedding, insisting Della was not the killer. To prove that, she was willing to help me find out who was. We'd start with a visit to the hospital before work. Maybe the police wouldn't be there at that early hour.

I swung by her apartment to pick her up at seven o'clock. As much as Rubie hated early mornings, I was pleasantly surprised to see her ready and waiting for me by her complex's front door. She must really want to rule out Della. Not as badly as I wanted to clear Claire, however.

She opened the car door, and a surge of Love's Baby Soft billowed into the car before she did. I wrinkled up my nose. I learned to tolerate it much better than I used to, but I had a long way to go before liking it.

"So what's the plan?" she said as soon as she closed the door.

"Your seatbelt for starters," I said, waiting for her to buckle up.

"Cut me some slack. I may look together on the outside, but I'm still half asleep on the inside. Coffee, coffee, coffee. I need coffee."

As soon as I heard the click of her belt, I took off. "We'll hit the coffee cart in the lobby first thing," I said.

Neither of us was chatty on the drive. Rubie and Claire were both extroverts. Their thoughts took all of half a second to tumble out of their mouths. I assumed Rubie was quiet only because it was early morning, and I was okay with that. I took advantage of the quiet to plot our visit.

The hospital parking lot was nearly empty. Visiting hours didn't begin until eight, so getting to his room, especially in Intensive Care, would be the first big hurdle.

As I promised Rubie, we swung by the coffee cart first thing then slipped into the elevator, calling as little attention to ourselves as possible, which wasn't easy. People tended to notice Rubie no matter where she was or what she was wearing. Tall, blond, blue-eyed, spunky.

We made it to the sixth floor without getting stopped. I felt like I was the criminal rather than trying to catch one. As I had feared, the doors to the Intensive Care Unit were locked. Beside the door was a button to push for attention. Precisely what we were trying to avoid.

I took a deep breath and said, "Here goes nothin'."

"Wait!" Rubie whispered, her hand pressing against my arm. "What are we going to say? They're not just going to buzz us in."

"Maybe whoever is at the desk will be distracted with something else and unlock the door," I said, pushing the button. It wasn't like me at all to not have everything planned to the last detail. The time crunch made me sloppy, and I hoped it didn't cost us some valuable information.

"Can I help you?" came a voice, sounding tinny through the tiny speaker.

"We're here to see Mr. Frost," I said.

"I'm his niece," Rubie said.

Startled, I stared at her with wide eyes.

"I'm his only family," she added.

I slapped her arm with the back of my hand. What if he had family and they'd already been to see him?

"Visiting hours don't start for another hour, ma'am. You'll need to come back or have a seat in the family waiting room."

"Please," she said, sounding so close to tears she almost had me convinced. "I have to be to work at eight, and if I'm late, my boss will fire me. She's super strict and has been waiting for a chance to get rid of me." I elbowed her hard and shot her a look, and she grinned. "My uncle depends on my income," she said, rubbing her arm where my elbow hit.

It was so quiet for a moment that any hope I had of getting in plummeted.

"Come on in," the woman finally said as the door buzzed open.

I grabbed it before it had a chance to lock again. "You think because you're cute, you can get away with anything you want."

"You're the one who's forcing me to be here."

"I'm doing no such thing," I argued.

"In order to clear Della—"

"And Claire."

"And Claire," she agreed. "Let's get this done—"

"Melanie Hogan," a man's voice said behind me.

I froze and turned to see Detective Walker. Next, I quickly glanced at the nurse's desk. As luck would have it, one nurse focused on the white scheduling board behind the counter, and the other disappeared into one of the rooms.

"Detective Walker," I said, not quite meeting his eyes. My cheeks warmed.

"I certainly hope you're not getting involved in my investigation."

"Of course not," Rubie blurted. "We're here to see my uncle."

"And who would that be?" he asked.

"You wouldn't know him," she said.

Man! She was good at this! She didn't even bat an eye, and her voice was steady as a big oak tree.

"Try me," he said.

Rubie paused, probably searching for the most plausible answer. His eyes locked on hers until his phone buzzed. That was three hurdles we'd cleared in the past fifteen minutes. Surely that meant that the Big Guy was leading us through this. Which meant it was the right thing to do. *Right*?

Walker squinted at the screen on his phone. "Look, ladies, I've got to take this." He held up a finger toward me. "Stay out of my investigation." Then he winked at Rubie. "If your uncle is Mr. Frost, he's asleep. Stay out."

The minute he took his call outside the ICU, I said to Rubie, "He was totally flirting with you!"

"Was not!" she argued.

We peeked in the rooms as we crept down the hall.

"You're the ones here to see Mr. Frost?"

We turned to see the nurse who was behind the desk writing on the whiteboard a moment ago.

"Yes," Rubie said. "Terrible, terrible thing that happened to my uncle. I sure hope they catch the guy who did this."

A corner of my lips curved upward. Rubie missed her calling as an actress. I was proud of her, yes I was.

"Don't you worry, honey," the nurse said. "We're keeping him sedated but working him out of it as safely as possible. He's been in and out of consciousness. More in than out. And his memory is a bit fuzzy. But trust you me, it will only be a matter of time before he's able to identify the monster who put him in here."

"I hope you're right," Rubie fretted. "I just don't know what I would ever do without him."

The nurse patted Rubie's shoulder. "You don't worry about that, sweetie. We have the best staff here to help him get well." She walked as she talked, so we followed her — right to Nick's room.

She left us alone, and we opened the sliding glass door. It was dark in Nick's room. The hum of the ventilator and beeping of several machines echoed in the otherwise silence. It was eerie.

I examined the room, taking everything in. Nick's eyes were closed. With our time already limited due to Walker being in the area and Nick sleeping during the narrow window of time, it appeared our luck had run out. I sighed.

"It was worth a shot," I said, feeling defeated. We'd gotten this far for nothing.

"Sorry, Mel," Rubie said, pulling me toward the door. "Come on before Walker comes back and sees us in here."

As we turned to leave, I heard a faint sound from Nick's bed. I spun around to look. His eyes were barely open, and he was trying to talk, the ventilator making it impossible. I hustled to his side, Rubie right behind me.

"Hey, Nick," I said softly. "My name is Melanie, and this is Rubie." I nodded toward her. "I'm the one who found you and called the police." He blinked slowly one time and nodded ever so slightly. "Nick, do you know who did this to you?" Nothing. "Maybe you can blink once for yes and twice for no?" One blink. Good! Now to speed things up before Walker came back in. I leaned closer to Nick. "Nick, do you know who did this to you?" One slow, sleepy blink. My heart sped up a bit. I cursed my lack of planning as I, yet, again, forgot my notebook. I scanned the room, frantically searching for a piece of paper. Unless I used his medical chart or the dry erase board that listed the people's names on his care team for this shift and the no food by mouth order. *No kidding!* That they needed to put that up there when he had a ventilator was a little unnerving. I was out of luck.

Rubie elbowed me and leaned close to my ear. "Try giving him some names."

"Della Birk?" I said. And gasped when Rubie's elbow made a connection with my ribs.

"Was it a man?" I asked, rubbing my side. One lazy blink. Despite hearing a man's voice when I was at the farmhouse, I decided to ask anyway. The man I heard might have had an accomplice. "Howard Lewis?" I held my breath when he blinked, then let it out when the second blink followed. "Donny—" I looked at Rubie. "What is Donny's last name?" She stared at me blankly. "Della's husband."

"What is it with you wanting to connect this whole debacle with Della somehow?" Rubie whispered harshly.

"Della used to be an under-the-table Oxy supplier. There were Oxy pills by Patti's body."

"And you just automatically assume this is related to Patti?"

"She admitted to being Patti's supplier," I said in a hushed tone.

"That doesn't mean Della killed her!" Rubie shot back.

"Rubie!" I said, the urgency in my tone palpable. "We're kind of in a hurry here." Nick's eyes were beginning to close.

"West. Donny West."

Nick's eyes opened again. He blinked. And then another slow blink.

"Trudy Flynn?" I asked.

"He said it was a man," Rubie said.

I kept my eyes on Nick, who blinked once. I waited for the second one, but it didn't come. "Was it Trudy Flynn, Nick? Is that who did this to you?"

A look of frustration clouded over his eyes. He blinked. Once.

"What are you ladies doing here?"

I shot upright, and my breath caught. Walker! I met Rubie's eyes. Darn it! I hurried to come up with a story.

"We left Rubie's uncle's room when he fell asleep," I said. "We noticed Nick on our way out and thought we'd pop in and see how he's doing. You know, since I'm the one who found him and all. Just to be sure he's doing okay." Nick's eyes closed again. "So I guess we'll be going then."

Walker's eyes narrowed as his gaze darted from Rubie to me then back to Rubie. "You never did tell me the name of your uncle."

"His name is, uh, his name is John—"

A new nurse came into the room. "There are too many people in here," she said, then settled her attention on Rubie and me. "Ladies, you'll have to leave now."

I exhaled my relief. "Come on, Rubie," I said, taking her by the arm. "You heard the nurse. We'd better leave." I turned to look behind me as we turned the corner. "Good luck, Walker. You take care now."

Rubie and I hurried straight for the door with the buzzer and pushed through it before Walker could say another word. Unless he chased us down. Which I was sure he wouldn't. But I was equally sure I'd be getting a call from Levi after Walker talked to him.

24

We didn't bother waiting by the bank of elevators for fear Walker would catch up with us. I wanted to buy some time before having to answer to him. Instead, we took the stairs down two floors and then hopped on the elevator from there and finished our descent.

As soon as we got outside, Rubie said, "What do you make of that?"

I shook my head. "I don't know yet."

"I mean, he blinked once when you asked if it was a man. But also blinked once when you said Trudy's name."

"I know. I was there."

She skimmed right over my sarcasm, a trait I admired about both her and Claire. "Maybe we missed the second blink when you asked if it was a man."

"No, I'm sure of it. I watched him like none other. I wonder…" I trailed off as I turned over scenarios in my head.

"Maybe he's not entirely sure who it was," she said.

My phone rang just as we reached the car.

"Aren't you gonna answer that?" Rubie asked.

"No. It's too cold to take my mittens off. Besides," I muttered, "it's Levi."

"Oh, man!" she exclaimed as we slid into my car. "Walker didn't waste any time calling him."

"You sound surprised," I said. "Maybe we should pay Trudy a visit after work."

"We have the Secret Santa reveal party this evening," Rubie said.

"Darnit! That's right." I'd forgotten about that.

"You've already rescheduled it once, Mel. You can't reschedule again. Especially on such short notice."

"Yeah, that wouldn't be good, would it." It was a statement, not a question. The ladies deserved better than to be put off another day. We always had a fun time. And we had Stormi's sensational cupcakes to look forward to. I glanced at my watch. Seven-forty-five. "What time is your first appointment?" I put the car in reverse and stepped on the gas.

"Dang!" she exclaimed as she grabbed the dash. "Nine-thirty. And I'd like to make it alive."

"I have one at nine. We can make it to Trudy's if we go right now."

"We don't know where she lives," Rubie said, looking at me as though I'd lost my marbles.

I smiled at her victoriously and winked. "Yeah, we do."

"But how —"

"I have my ways."

"But I thought —"

"It's a little scary to realize how easy it is to get personal information from the internet."

"Are you going to let me finish a sentence?" she asked, exasperated.

"Sorry." And I was. It was a bad habit of mine. "Do you mind if we stop? I promise it won't take long. We're only five minutes away."

Rubie sighed. "Go for it. Just have us to the salon by nine and not a second later. And you're going to have to drive me home after the reveal party since we won't have time to go get my car before work."

"Deal." Despite Nick's answer confusing me, I felt like we were making some good headway.

Less than five minutes later, we pulled up in front of a sage-colored two-story house with eggshell-colored trim. Rubie opened her car door before I fully stopped.

"Whoa there, Petunia," I said.

"We're in a hurry."

I nodded. "That we are, but our chances of safely getting to the salon hinges on not jumping from a moving car."

Rubie snickered. "We were going one mile per hour. What was I going to do, break a nail?"

We strode side-by-side up the sidewalk, both taking a giant step over a drifted bank, not an easy feat in heeled boots.

I pressed the doorbell but didn't hear anything, so I knocked and waited. When no one answered, Rubie knocked harder. Still nothing.

"Maybe I can take a break sometime during the day and try again," I said.

"Yeah, right," she scoffed. "If you can take a break long enough to breathe, I will be impressed. We're booked solid."

She had a point. In the days before Christmas, we overlapped appointments. Sometimes there wasn't even time to cram food down our pie-holes.

We'd just turned back toward the car when I heard the faint *tap-tap-tap* of heels on what sounded like a tile floor. My gaze darted toward Rubie and then back to the door as it whisked open.

"Yeah?" Trudy said through the glass in the storm door.

My breath caught in my throat. A long scratch ran across her forehead. I swallowed hard. Could it be? But it was a man's voice. I'd swear to it.

"Hi, Trudy. I'm Melanie Hogan from A Cut Above."

"Yeah, I know who you are. I was there for free haircut day. As if you don't remember." Her tone was anything but friendly or welcoming.

"This is Rubie," I tilted my head toward her. "Do you have a minute?"

"Not really," Trudy said. "I'm running late as it is."

"Just two minutes?" I asked. "I promise I won't take any longer than that."

She looked at her watch, then behind her before she unlocked the door and opened it.

"Alright, then." She stepped aside to let us in. "But make it snappy."

"What happened to your face?" I asked.

"What happened to yours?" she snapped back without missing a beat.

So that's how this was going to go. "Do you know Nick Frost?" I asked, getting right to it.

"Why do you want to know?"

"Because someone stopped Nick from playing Santa at the Christmas Festival. And I think the same person had something to do with Patti's death."

"What's that got to do with me?" Her umber-colored eyes were festering embers.

"I was hoping maybe you could tell me that," I said.

"You came to my house to accuse me of something, Melanie?"

"I'm not accusing you of anything. I just asked if you know Nick Frost."

Rubie stood beside me, one hand on the door handle.

"Not personally."

"Can I ask where you were two evenings ago?"

"You can, but it doesn't mean I'll tell you. It's none of your business."

She held my gaze, unflinching and hard. She was not going to make this easy. But then why would she?

"We're dancing in circles, Trudy, so why don't I just come right to the point."

"Yes," she said as enjoyment now flickered in her eyes, "why don't you?"

"We both know you and Patti Parker weren't friends, and—"

"I don't think anyone was friends with that moron," she said. "So if you're accusing me of killing her...well, let's just say if you accused everyone who didn't like Patti of killing her, the jails would be full in every city anywhere close to Birch Haven."

"So you knew Patti, who was murdered, and you know Nick, who—"

"Know?" she asked. What appeared to be relief edged out the irritation in her eyes from mere moments before.

"Yes, *know* him. He's still alive." I watched her carefully. "Where'd you get the scratch on your forehead, Trudy? Were you at Nick's house two evenings ago chasing me through the woods in the back of his house? We're both sporting the same facial decorations. Those branches and twigs can be brutal on the skin, huh?"

Her gaze darted in back of her down the hallway that led to the door. She frowned and touched her forehead. "I was playing with my friend's kid's cat. It didn't like me so well."

"Not very original," I said.

"Norman?" she called.

"Yeah, darlin'?" came a man's voice from upstairs.

"Come down here, please? And be sure you're dressed. We have company."

"Who is it?" He called.

"Melanie Hogan and friend."

"Rubie," Rubie said. "The friend has a name. I'm Rubie."

Trudy ignored her, keeping her gaze steady on me. Behind her, coming up the hallway was the man from the phone store. This was Norman? I hadn't gotten a look at the woman who was with him. She had been dressed like an Eskimo and standing on the other side of this hulk of a man. And when I left, she was looking at the phone case display with her back toward me. He vaguely resembled the photos on social media, but a much larger version. He'd put on some serious pounds around his middle since those pictures were taken.

"We meet again," Norman said, extending his hand, which I didn't shake. He shrugged disinterestedly. "What seems to be the problem here?" He placed a meaty hand on Trudy's back.

"She knows," Trudy muttered.

"Is that so." The trace of a smile contradicted eyes of steel.

"But Nick's alive," she said to Norman. "That's great news, huh?"

For hearing what she considered good news, her tone didn't portray it.

"It all makes sense now," I said, feeling Rubie's attention on me.

"It, um, does?" Rubie stammered.

"It does," I repeated. I looked at Norman. "You used to date Patti. It's no secret that Patti and Trudy weren't friends. As an onlooker, I think it's safe to say there was pretty intense hostility between the two." I turned my attention to Trudy. "Wouldn't you say that's a true statement?"

"There was hostility between Patti and half the town," Trudy scoffed.

"Yes, but half the town didn't date your husband. Patti did."

Trudy waved a hand in dismissal. "For Pete's sake, that was eons ago."

I raised my eyebrows in question as I looked at Norman. "Was it, Norman? Eons ago. Or was it more recent?"

Redness crept up his neck just above the collar of his white t-shirt and interspersed with the stubble on his neck and chin. As if he could feel it, he stroked his chin with his free hand.

"You women just love to start trouble, don't you?" His tone matched his eyes. "Well, it's not going to work here."

"So you're saying you haven't seen Patti anytime recently?"

"What is she talking about, Norman?" Trudy asked.

"Close the door," he ordered Rubie. When Rubie didn't move, he said louder, "I said close the door."

Rubie jumped and turned to leave, grabbing my arm tight, nails digging into my sleeve as she did, pulling me with her.

"We have to be going," she said.

In one fell swoop, Norman stepped around us and slammed the door shut. I jumped. Rubie's fingers pressed hard through my coat, pinching my arm.

"Norman, what is she talking about?" Trudy said, her voice louder. "What's this about Patti?"

"Do you want me to tell her, Norman?" I asked. "About the note you wrote to Patti on her baking contest certificate? Or do you want to tell her yourself?"

"What are you doing?" Rubie hissed, her head close to mine.

"Let Rubie go, Norman," I said. "You're not upset with her. It's me you're mad at."

"What is going on?" Trudy blurted. "Someone tell me! I thought this was about Nick. It was a simple fight between two grown men. Norman told me all about it. What happened to Nick was an accident. Tell them, Norman," she said. "And since he's alive, there's nothing to worry about."

Norman glanced at his wife, and Rubie reached for the door again. Norman was faster and had a hand on each of our arms, leading us further into the house. Panic edged its way in. *Way to go, Melanie.* But the pieces of the jigsaw puzzle fit into place. Patti taunting Trudy about her husband. The note on the certificate. The unique hitch in Santa's gait that I noticed as he ran across the parking lot from Cole. What I didn't know was the why. If Trudy killed Patti, how was Norman involved? I had a feeling I was about to find out.

"Trudy, go upstairs," Norman ordered, his gaze not leaving Rubie and me.

"Not until you tell me what she meant about Patti, the plastic bimbo. What note, for God's sake. Are we still in high school?"

"Trudy," Norman growled.

"I said, no." She stood her ground close to the door.

Given her level of defiance, it was clear she wasn't afraid of him, which gave me some comfort.

"I gave up everything for you," Trudy said to Norman in a voice of steel. "I trusted you." She threw her hand in my direction. "And apparently she knows something I should probably know. It's time you come clean with me, hubs."

"Darlin', please," Norman said, his eyes softening as he glanced at Trudy. "I'm begging you. Go upstairs. I'll tell you everything later. I promise."

His eyes steeled again when he looked at me.

"So there *is* something to tell?" Trudy asked. "You've been cheating on me with that—that—floozy? How could you!"

Before I knew what had happened, she hiked an arm back and hurled a shoe at him. It skimmed past his head as he ducked, the heel sticking into the drywall. I knew which to be more afraid of between the two. And it wasn't Norman.

25

I slid a hand into my handbag, my fingers fumbling around for my phone or my gun, whichever I found first. Rubie gasped when Trudy produced a sleek little handgun from a drawer in the entryway table in the foyer. My breath caught while I frantically felt the buttons on my phone, guessing at the one that held Levi on speed dial.

"I trusted you, Norman," Trudy said, pointing the gun from Rubie and me to Norman. She jerked it toward the chair that sat caddy-corner to the sofa Rubie and I sat on. "Sit down, Norman." She appeared as one who'd consumed far too much caffeine. Her eyes were insanely wide, staccato speech, and quick, jerky movements.

"Trudy, what has gotten into you?" he asked.

"What's gotten into *me*?" she screeched.

"Hello? Hello? Melanie?" Levi's faint voice came from the phone in my purse. Thank the good Lord I'd hit the right button.

Trudy's head snapped to look at me. "What was that?" She noticed my hand in my purse. "Crap!" she exclaimed, looking suddenly panicked. She bolted across the room, snapped my purse from my lap, and tossed it to the floor and out of my reach.

"Levi!" I yelled. "Trudy and Norman Flynn! They killed Patti and tried to kill Nick!"

Trudy's hand that held the gun cracked against my cheek. So much for the Dermabond being a success. I gingerly touched my cheek, feeling the warm stickiness of blood. *If Trudy does away with us, at least my blood will produce evidence that I was here*, I thought. That, however, brought little to no comfort.

"Melanie!" Rubie screamed, instantly assessing the damage before Trudy ordered her back.

"Levi and the entire police department are on their way, Trudy," I said, holding my cheek. "You won't get away with this."

"No, *he* won't get away with this," she spat, jerking her gun toward Norman. Her nostrils flared. "You're pathetic," she told him. "Pathetic! You think she liked you? She was only trying to get back at me. That's what Patti did. That's what she's always done!"

I almost felt sorry for him. Almost. As she continued to emasculate him, he shrank further into the chair cushion, his chest deflating.

"Why?" I asked him, needing to know the part I still couldn't figure out.

"Yes, Norman, why?" Trudy asked, all her attention on him now.

Rubie could have made a run for it, and Trudy wouldn't have even noticed.

"Why what?" Norman asked weakly.

"Stop playing dumb," Trudy said. "Why'd you try to kill Nick?"

"I didn't," he said. "I told you that. It was a fight between two men. Nick lost."

"You didn't try to kill him?" I asked in disbelief. "Because he barely pulled through. He's not out of the woods yet."

Three sets of eyes were on him, waiting for the explanation.

"I thought something sounded fishy," Trudy accused, glaring at Norman. "Nick can't even bump into someone without offering an apology, much less get into a fistfight."

"Trudy, baby, we need to get out of here. The cops are on their way."

She shrugged. "Sad for you. I haven't done anything wrong."

"You're the one with the gun, baby." He held his hand out, palm up. "Give me the gun."

"Self-defense," she said, devoid of emotion now. She had de-escalated as quickly as she escalated minutes earlier. "And I'm not your baby. Not anymore. I'll say you came at me—us," she said, flashing the gun toward Rubie and me again before pointing it back at Norman.

He sighed, then said, "It wasn't supposed to happen that way with Nick. I asked him to let me take his place at the Christmas festival and he wouldn't. I told him I was going to regardless of what he said, and he grabbed the phone to call the police."

"So the story you told me about the fight was bogus."

Her hostility chilled me to the core. And yet I pitied her.

"Why?" Trudy yelled. "Why the sudden need to play Santa Claus? A long-lost childhood dream?"

"Patti said she was gonna tell you, and there was nothing I could do about it. I couldn't let her do that, Trudy. I had to keep my eye on her. I couldn't let her ruin us. Me and you." His eyes pleaded with her to understand.

Trudy scoffed. "She didn't have to, you idiot. You did a good enough job of that all on your own."

"Darlin', it didn't mean anything. It was only one time, and I told her it was never going to happen again. That I love my wife. She knew you were going to be at the festival so—"

"How?"

"How?" he asked, eyes clouded with confusion. "What do you mean?"

"How did she know I would be at the festival?"

"I might have told her," he choked.

"You told her?" she screeched. "How dare you talk about me to your lover! Why would you do that?"

"I don't know. It just came up."

"Yes, we've found that out."

I choked back a laugh and coughed to try to cover it up. Rubie made a quiet snorting sound like she does when she's trying to keep from giggling. Given Trudy's comment, we weren't the only ones to see the irony of his answer.

"Norman," I said, "I'm curious. Why did you go back to Nick's? The evening I was there. Why were you there?"

"Because as stupid as he is," Trudy said, "despite what this dingbat did," she stabbed the gun in the air toward Norman, "he wanted to be sure the guy was okay. That he wasn't dead."

I looked at Norman. "But if you were there to help Nick, why did you chase me away and then leave?"

"Oh my Lord!" she exclaimed, clearly exasperated. She wasn't about to let Norman speak for himself. She held the gun and was taking full advantage of the power. "You're as dumb as he is! You think he was going to let you see him and then hang around and shoot the breeze until your boyfriend got there to arrest him?"

Her adrenaline was ramping up and it was a tad scary. Her attention was once again entirely on Norman. The hand holding the gun shook slightly. I sure hoped the police got here fast, or she would inadvertently pull the trigger.

As if on cue, sirens sounded, getting louder quickly, piercing the room and my eardrums, until they were in the front yard. Trudy's gun never strayed from Norman. I could have even run by now, and she probably wouldn't have stopped me. If she noticed at all. But what was the point? The police were here. Telling Claire she no longer had to worry about being a suspect would be a Christmas gift for both of us.

***

By the time the scene was secured and processed, Trudy arrested for the murder of Patti Parker and Norman for the attempted murder of Nick Frost, it was past opening time at the salon. Rubie and I gave our statements to the police, and a paramedic re-glued my cheek and gave me an iced gel pack. I was going to have quite the bruise. I made a brief call to Claire earlier to let her know we would be late but didn't give her any specifics. Just that I had the best news of her life when I arrived.

"So much for getting me back to the salon not a minute later than nine," Rubie said as we trotted to my car.

"You know I'm a lady of my word and would have if it was at all possible."

"Yeah, yeah, I know. I can't even argue with you there."

Right before I opened my car door, I remembered something for which I wanted an answer.

"I'll be right back," I told Rubie.

"Loverboy is busy; leave him alone," Rubie said as she plopped down in the car and slammed her door shut.

Levi was busy, no doubt. Apparently, since Claire was no longer a suspect, they allowed him to help in whatever limited capacity they deemed appropriate. But it wasn't Levi with whom I wanted to talk.

Norman was sitting in the back of a police car, handcuffed. Two officers stood in the front of the vehicle on the driver's side, deep in conversation. I snuck around the back of the car on Norman's side and bent over to speak through the cracked open window.

"Norman, what I'm dying to know—pardon the pun—is why you told Trudy about Nick's assault. If you didn't want her to know why you needed to be at the Christmas festival, why risk telling her about it at all?"

He sighed and shook his head slowly, looking straight ahead. "Honesty's the best policy. I didn't want to keep it from her."

Surely I'd misheard. I swallowed a laugh and quickly glanced at the two officers.

"Honesty?" I said. "Like how honest you were with her about Patti?"

"I would have told her eventually. When the time was right." He widened his eyes. "But you had to butt in and ruin things." He shook his head and muttered, "Women!"

Something felt off, but I couldn't pinpoint what it was. Yet.

"Why did you run at the festival?"

"I heard Trudy say 'Oh, my God,' and thought she recognized me."

I frowned and shook my head. *Was this guy for real?* "And running would have made her forget?"

He coughed, catching the attention of the officers.

"Ms. Hogan," one of them said, "step away from the suspect."

Oops. I smiled, waved, and trotted over to my car.

"It's about dang time," Rubie scolded. "We're not ladies of leisure, you know. We have jobs. Clients depending on us."

"Did we switch places here or what?" I asked, giving her a sidelong glance as I started the motor. Usually, I was the ultra-responsible one. "Now we know why Nick blinked once when I said Trudy's name. Even though she's a woman, he recognized the last name. Flynn. That's what he was saying yes to."

"So he and Norman must know each other."

"Yeah, they must. I'd like to know how."

Rubie shrugged, turned up the fan for the heater, and said, "Well, regardless, at least they caught him. That poor old man. Breaks my heart."

"Yeah," I agreed. "Bet he didn't realize being Santa was such a dangerous job."

26

It was a little after ten when Rubie and I got to the salon. The ladies managed to reschedule our first clients for the end of the day, bumping our Secret Santa reveal party back a half hour. From Bab's account, Rubie's client appeared to be far more understanding than mine.

"Which means by the time I finish with my client, I will be more than ready to have a cocktail and a cupcake," I told her.

Babs grimaced. "Gross! Only you would think of putting those two things together."

I nodded. "Yeah, pretty much."

By the looks Claire kept giving me, I couldn't wait to tell her the news any more than she could wait to hear it. We kept an eye on each other's progress, trying desperately to schedule a short break at the same time, even if it was for two measly minutes.

And when that break eventually happened, and we were able to escape to the office at two-fifteen, it was worth the wait. As soon as I relayed a brief description of the encounter—the more detailed one would have to wait until the party after work—Claire stood still as a statue as she absorbed all that I said. She didn't even blink.

And then the widest grin ever crossed her face, revealing that charming gap between her front teeth. Her arms shot up in the air, fists pumped. She squealed and then swept me up in a hug—all within a matter of a millisecond.

"We're okay!" I called out to the others as soon as I could extricate myself and catch a breath. I wasn't sure I would be able to hear well for the rest of the day, however. Not to mention the excruciating pain in my cheek. "Merry Christmas," I said to her. "Now, let's go finish this day so we can celebrate with the girls after work."

She stopped and turned when she got to the door. "You know, this doesn't excuse you doing stupid stuff, almost getting yourself killed. Again. Just sayin'. And you might want to take five to hold that ice pack on your face again."

"You're welcome," I said, grinning.

Between the holiday hair color clients, women sitting under dryers in rollers, cuts and styles in and out, even some perm clients, the afternoon zipped by in a blur of activity. Laughter, incessant chatter, Christmas music, hair spray, and the pleasing odor of colors, perm solutions, and artificial nails filled the air. Everything was perfect.

Until it wasn't.

An exchange between Norman and Trudy niggled at my thoughts. *Trudy hadn't known about Norman and Patti until today. If that was her motive, it wouldn't have been so at the time of the murder.*

***

Babs and Connie finished early and ran home to change into something more comfortable for our party. Claire decided to run a couple of errands since she had some time to blow. Cole was staying with Sydney for the evening. Remarkable progress.

"Melanie," Claire said as she wrapped her scarf around her neck and slipped her gloves on before going outside, "Sydney didn't even seem to mind."

"She shouldn't," I said. "Cole spoils her. And you've been dating long enough for Pete's sakes."

"Sometimes those things take a while, honey," my client, Marie, said. "They eventually just fall into place."

"She resisted it for the longest time, you know?" Claire said.

297

"Cole striving so hard to prove he's not coming between the two of you helped, too, don't you think?"

"Totally!" Claire said.

"Sounds like you've got yourself a good one, Claire," Marie said.

"Yeah." Claire grinned and headed for the door. "I think I'll keep him."

"If you don't, someone else will," Rubie called out.

Levi came in the door just as my last client left. Every time I saw him in his black leather coat, black gloves, and black cop beanie, my heart fluttered. The man had utterly captured my heart.

"Perfect timing," I said, standing on my tiptoes to plant a light kiss on his lips.

"Can we take it in the office?" he asked.

"I don't have time," I teased. "We have our Secret Santa reveal."

His eyes twinkled their amusement. "To talk."

I looked at Rubie, whose client was filling her in on her Christmas plans. "I'll be in the back, Rubie."

I led the way, Levi following. He closed the door, leaving it open just a crack.

"I'm assuming you told Claire," he said.

I grinned. "I did. She was over-the-moon elated." My earlier thought re-surfaced. "How certain are you that Trudy is responsible for Patti's murder?"

His eyes held mine, his narrowing slightly after a moment. "Why?"

"Something occurred to me this afternoon."

"And that would be?" When I didn't answer right away, he said, "They released her from custody because we didn't have anything solid to hold her on. We only have circumstantial evidence. No proof. Of course, she's maintaining her innocence. But every criminal does. Walker thinks she's good for it."

I stared at him for a minute, not really seeing him. "Levi," I said, "Trudy didn't know about Norman's affair with Patti until today."

He exhaled long and slow and ran his hand over his bald head. "It was clear they weren't friends, so —
"

"By the sounds of things, I'm not sure anyone was friends with Patti. If we're looking at people who — "

"We?" he said, giving me the old stink-eye. "I thought we were done with this."

At the sound of a knock on the door, I said, "Come in, Rubie."

"How'd you know it was me?" she asked as she pushed the door open.

I stared at her for a minute, at a loss for words. "Since you're the only one here, I'm going to pretend you didn't just ask me that."

"Whatever." She chuckled, a quiet, tired sound. "Not one of my brightest moments. It's just been a long, exhausting day."

"Hey, Rubie, what are your thoughts about Trudy as the killer?"

She thought about it and frowned. "I want to say yes, but I can't."

"Why?" Levi asked.

"What's her motive? Disliking Patti? Everyone did," she said, hands out, palms up.

"So I've heard," Levi grumbled.

"You asked, I told," Rubie said with a shrug.

"Della was Patti's Oxy supplier and cut her off. Made Patti pretty mad, and she threatened to turn Della in," I said.

Rubie shook her head vigorously. "There you go with Della again. I'm telling you Della is innocent. She's not capable of murder."

"What about her overprotective brother, then?"

Levi looked back and forth from me to Rubie as we discussed the possibilities, but he stayed quiet.

"What are you thinking?" I asked him.

"That Walker is the lead on this case, and he's looked at everything. He thinks Trudy is his gal."

I stared at him absently again, then shook my head slowly. "I've just got this feeling..." It was quiet for a second before I said, "Hey, how did Nick and Norman know each other?"

"How do you know they did?" Levi asked.

"When we were talking with Nick this morning—"

"Yeah, about that…" His eyes narrowed as he looked at me.

"We were there; I won't even try to deny it."

Levi shook his head and chuckled. "Go on."

"Well, we had this blink once for yes, twice for no agreement with Nick. He knew his attacker. How were they connected, do you know?"

"Nick was a substitute teacher at Birch Haven High while Norman and Trudy were students there."

I nodded as I pondered his answer. "Hmm. Good to know his life aspiration wasn't just to play Santa." I peered at Levi. "Any more news on the poison that killed Patti?"

"Not that I've heard."

"Well, get on it, man," I said, grinning. "What good is it having an in at the police department if I can't get the inside scoop?"

He smiled and stood. "With that, I'm out. You ladies have a fun night tonight. And behave. We're short-staffed at the police department."

"You hear that, Rubie? Behave tonight," I said.

The sound of Levi's laughter nearly drowned out Rubie's "Yeah, right!" comment.

I walked him to the door. As Levi left, Claire came in, followed by Babs and Connie.

"You ladies ready to get this thing going?" I said, locking the door behind them.

"I've got the wine," Babs said, holding up a bottle in each hand. "We still have a few plastic flutes tucked in the back of the cabinet next to the washer and dryer."

"Oh, shoot! That reminds me!" I said, slapping my hand against my forehead. I winced and groaned when it reminded me of one of my casualties. "I have to run down and get the cupcakes from Stormi's walk-in cooler. I'll be right back." I raced for the office to grab my coat. When I returned to the salon area, none of them appeared overly thrilled with my trip for the goods.

"None for me," Connie said with a grimace, hand on her stomach. "After all the junk food I've grazed on today, I don't think I'll look at anything sweet for weeks. How do you expect me to keep this svelte figure?" She ran her hands down along her voluptuous bosom and hips.

Babs laughed and agreed. "Yeah, I can't look at anything sweet right now. I stopped for gas on my way back here, and they were giving out free hot cocoa. Of course, I had to have one after everything else I've eaten today." She shook her head. "I don't know why I do that to myself."

"Like you have anything to worry about," Connie said. "My broom handle is wider than you and Melanie put together."

"Hey!" Rubie said. "Why am I not included in that? You think I'm fat, don't you?"

"That doesn't even warrant an answer," Connie said as she jerked her sleeve down.

I rolled my eyes at Rubie's need for validation. Of all of us, she had the most desirable figure. As in perfect. Men gawked at her, and women envied her.

"What I want to know is how you can be so insecure," I said, shaking my head. "Do you or Claire want the cupcakes?" I said, looking between the two of them before putting my coat on.

"Nope."

"Not me," they said.

"But they're so cute," I protested. "Seriously, the cutest Christmas cupcakes I've ever seen. In magazines, even!"

"No," they all said emphatically.

I put my hands up. "Okay! No need to get all huffy ya'all. I'll go over there tomorrow and pick them up. What's one more day."

"Gives 'day-old' a whole new meaning," Claire said.

"They've been in the cooler this whole time," I said. "They'll still be superb."

"I want to get to the presents," Rubie said, grinning. "Come on." She led the way over to the Christmas tree in the waiting area, turning to look over her shoulder. "Hey, Mel, you didn't have my name, did you?"

"The secret part is still secret at this point," I said. "Why, are you afraid?"

"Very," she said, plunking down in the chair next to the tree before falling to her knees and bending over to scoop the presents from beneath it. I smacked her on the hind end, and she screamed. "That's why I'm afraid if you have my name," she said. "Because you're just evil."

27

Rubie finished pawing all five gifts out from under the tree and then sat back on her heels. A chunk of hair that had snagged on a pine branch hung over her eyes. She blew it out of the way, then clipped it again with the rest of her curls.

"This is crazy having to push the gifts way under there in the back," she said. "I vote next year we just hold onto 'em in the office until we're ready."

We tucked the gifts as far back as we could, because one year a couple of them went missing. This way, no one could nab one without making it a scene we would be sure to notice. Not that we went hog wild on our gifts to each other and it wouldn't be a massive loss if someone took one. They were more humorous and personal than valuable.

"You can't be trusted," I said, snickering. "You'll shake, rattle, and roll yours until you figure out what it is."

"I can't help it that I love presents," Rubie said, with the biggest grin and bright blue eyes twinkling.

"Poor Scott," I mumbled. "I hope he can afford you. Don't forget he only makes a police officer's salary."

We all settled in on the chairs by the tree, the magazine table in the center. I began straightening the magazines while Claire opened the bottle of Seven Deadly Zins. My favorite. She poured and handed me the first glass.

"How can you both be so—normal—after the events of this morning?" Claire asked, looking from me to Rubie, handing Rubie the second glass. "And you," she said to me, "your poor face!"

"Her face has been hurting me for a long time," Rubie said, laughing.

"Ha-ha!" I said, unable to stop from grinning.

"Fill Connie and me in," said Babs. "We're in the dark here."

"That's right!" I said, kicking my boots off and tucking my legs underneath me. "You guys don't know!"

I started at the beginning when Rubie and I went to the hospital to see Nick, pausing whenever Rubie chimed in from her perspective. By the time we finished, both Connie's and Bab's mouths hung open.

"How are the two of you still functioning after all that?" Connie asked.

"All in a day's work," I said with a chuckle, shaking my head slowly.

Rubie balled up one of the paper bags from the wine and tossed it my way. "It comes with the territory of being friends with Detective Melanie Hogan," she said. "Just a day in the life."

I laughed. I had to admit, once it was all said out loud, it did sound overwhelming. "I'll crash the minute I get home. My bed won't know what hit it."

"I'm so grateful I'm cleared from Patti's murder," Claire said, giving me a warm smile. "I'm not happy the way things went down, mind you," she added. "But I'm more grateful for the lengths the two of you went to for little ole' me."

"I did it for Syd," I teased. "Anyone want me to open the plate of cream cheese mints we got from the insurance company down the way?"

"Man, Melanie, how can you even think about food right now?" Connie groaned. "Seriously, you must have a bottomless pit for a stomach."

"I didn't say I wanted them," I said, defending my stomach. "Just that I would get them if anyone else wanted. Hey!" I said, remembering something, "would you guys have ever guessed Patti to be the kitchen kind?"

"Kitchen kind?" Claire asked.

"Yeah. Like a baker."

Rubie shrugged. "I didn't know her."

"Me either," the other three chimed in.

"I guess just knowing what little I do and her physical appearance, I wouldn't have expected it."

"How do you know she was?" Babs asked, running her hand over her spiked hair. It popped back up the minute she put her hand back down.

"I found a partial certificate stuck between the shelving and the wall in the restroom naming her as the winner of a contest. Must have fallen out of her bag with all the rest of her stuff."

"That is kind of odd," Babs agreed. "From what I've heard about her, I would have expected her to have hired kitchen staff rather than get her nails dirty."

"Exactly," I said.

"I don't care if she was a circus acrobat," Rubie said, sitting on the edge of her chair. "I want to open presents." She folded her hands together in a praying motion, glanced upward, and muttered, "Oh, please, oh, please, don't let Melanie have my name."

"You'd rather not have one at all?" I asked.

"I didn't say that," she said.

Connie laughed softly. "You two tease each other mercilessly. I'm surprised you're still friends."

Of all of us, Connie was the most unlike any of us. She was more reserved, even a bit shy, and didn't want anything whatsoever to do with any of our escapades. When I thought about it, it's a wonder that she'd stayed at the salon as long as she had.

"Melanie is like the sister I always wanted and never had," Rubie said as I dodged another paper ball from the second bag that she tossed at me. "We love to pick on each other, but I can trust her to keep me on the straight and narrow. If I ever do anything stupid, or am about to, she'll let me know about it. Her honesty is brutal sometimes, but it's always in my best interest." She snickered. "That's what I tell myself, anyway."

Emotion tugged at my heart, and I choked up. "Gee, Rubie, that was the sweetest thing you've ever said. I'm touched."

She waved a hand in dismissal. "Don't go all mushy on me. I just want to open presents. Even if you're the one who had my name."

She handed each gift to whoever's name was on the label. She lifted hers close to her ear and shook it. As she gave each of us our present, I guessed who had who's name. Claire's was long and narrow, tied at each end with curled ribbon. It didn't look like Rubie's style. Babs or Connie? Connie's gift was a rectangle, the size of a small shirt box, the paper littered with old-world style Santa's. I was certain

Claire had Connie's name. I scanned Rubie's, a metallic green bag with black paper sticking out the top. Hmm—It was Babs on that one. I knew who Babs's gift was from—*moi*.

"Oh my gosh!" Claire exclaimed, laughing. "You're totally deducing which gift is from whom. Give it a rest, girl!"

I gave her a sly grin. "Maybe." I held mine up, a pink, glitter bag with pink curled ribbon on the handles. "It doesn't take much creativity to guess who this one is from."

Rubie grinned. "Yeah, guess I should have at least tried to confuse you, huh?"

We opened gifts, ooh-ing and ahh-ing with dramatic gestures.

"Connie, you watch us as if we've all gone stark raving mad," I said, laughing. "You should be used to us by now."

"Really?" she said, scrunching up her face then smiling. "Is there such a thing as getting used to you crazy ladies?"

I shrugged. "You make a good point. But for the record, I used to be more normal before Rubie came along."

"Whatever!" Rubie said. "It's the wine. When you drink, you talk." She filled up my half-empty glass.

"Drink up. We want to know what dark secrets you have in there." She tapped her head with her finger.

"That's my cue to *stop* drinking," I said, setting my glass back down. I'd only had a glass and a half, but it was more than I usually drank. My drink of choice is the hard stuff—seltzer water with lemon or a slice of orange.

We joked, talked about some of our clients, our favorites, and the difficult ones we wouldn't mind traveling on to another salon. We laughed until we cried, and then it fell silent as we listened to "Grandma Got Run Over by a Reindeer" playing from the speakers in the ceiling.

"You know, this song is kind of morbid," I said. "Just sayin'." I glanced at my watch, then at each of the girls. "I hate to be the party-pooper, but I'm exhausted. And I have to bring Rubie home yet."

"I drive right by her place on my way home," Babs said. "I'll take her."

"You sure?" I asked.

"Of course. It'd be stupid for you to go out of your way for nothing."

"Excuse meee!" Rubie sang, standing and stomping her foot. "For *nothing*?"

Babs laughed as she stood up. "I guess that was a poor choice of words. You've had enough of Melanie for one day. Let me take you home."

"You're forgiven," Rubie said, trying unsuccessfully to pout. "Sorry, Mel," she said, hugging me, "I've had a safer offer."

I hugged her back. "Thanks, Rubie," I whispered in her ear before letting her go. "For everything."

"My pleasure, Nancy Drew."

One last squeeze and I gave her a little shove. "Go, smart alec."

Between the five of us, we had the wrapping paper, plastic flutes, wine bottles, and all evidence of a party picked up and put in their rightful places. Connie, Babs, and Rubie were out the door within five minutes, with Claire and I not more than a couple of minutes after that. I slid my key in the lock, clicked it into place, yanked on the handle once to be sure it was latched, and turned to leave.

"Hey, thanks again, Mel," Claire said. "You have no idea how much it means to me, what you did to clear my name."

I smiled and winked at her. Our breaths were white puffs of air. "Yeah, I do." I started walking with her to our cars and stopped. "Hey, I think I'm going to run and pick up those cupcakes and bring them to

Nana's for Christmas. The security guard was expecting me earlier anyway. He's working the night shift, so he'll still be there."

"Want me to come with you?"

"Nah. Go home to Sydney. She probably needs rescuing from that mean man of yours."

She laughed, her voice ringing out in the cold night air. "Yeah, right. Cole's the one who'll need rescuing."

"I'd never believe it, and no one else would either," I teased. "See ya tomorrow, hun."

"Bye, Mel."

28

I jogged as much as possible in my black heeled boots down the strip to the grocery store. By the time I reached the door, I'd wished I'd driven my car. It wasn't a long way, but at eight o'clock it was dark, and the cold pinched my cheeks and fingers. Foolishly, my mittens remained tucked away beside the center console in my car.

I'd just reached the door when my phone rang. I fumbled to get it out with numb fingers, dropping the darn thing before I could get it to my ear. A curse word escaped, and the security guard's head swiveled in my direction, a look of surprise on his face. I smiled at him sheepishly and held up a finger before answering my phone.

"Hello?"

"Hey, Blondie. What in the heck is going on there? Sounds like you're in a war zone."

I smiled into the phone at the sound of Levi's voice. "Hey," I said back. "Dropped my phone. My fingers are numb from the cold."

"Where are you? I thought you were at the salon."

"Party just ended. I ran to the grocery store to pick up some cupcakes Stormi left for me. The ladies didn't want anything sweet, so I thought I'd bring them to my grandmother's. Better than wasting them."

"Isn't the bakery long closed by now?"

"Yeah. Stan, the security guard, is bringing me to get them. Stormi already gave him permission."

"Feel like swinging by on your way home?" he asked.

"Ordinarily, I'd love to, but I'm so tired I'm not sure I'll make it to my bed before falling asleep. Raincheck?"

"If you're that tired, I'm not sure it's a good idea for you to drive all the way home."

"All the way?" I laughed softly. "It's fifteen minutes, twenty tops."

"It's just that—"

"What'd you call to tell me?"

"Do I need a reason to call, m'lady?"

"The fact that you called when you thought I was still at the party with the girls, yeah." I grinned.

"We found out the cause of Patti's death."

My eyes got huge, and I inhaled sharply in anticipation of what he would say next. When he didn't say anything, I said, "Are you seriously going to make me ask?"

"You'll never believe it."

"Try me."

"Looks like it was anaphylactic shock."

I took a moment to digest what he'd just said. Surely I'd misheard. "What?"

"Anaphylactic shock."

"But that means—it wasn't a homicide after all? That's great!"

"The autopsy showed she had peanut oil in her digestive system. Unless she drank it, which she wouldn't have done, it was murder."

"But how do you know—"

"Walker was able to locate her step-mother. Patti was allergic to peanuts. Carried an EpiPen everywhere she went."

"But there wasn't an EpiPen in her purse, was there?"

"Nope."

"Maybe it rolled under the shelving in the restroom along with Patti's certificate."

"What certificate?" he asked.

I realized that I hadn't told him about my discovery with everything that had been going on at the time, so I filled him in. As I talked, Stan, the security guard, paid close attention to my conversation, his brows knit in concern.

"You okay, Melanie?" he mouthed.

I nodded and gave him a weak smile. Someone murdered Patti with peanut oil? But who would have known she had a peanut allergy? It had to be someone who knew her pretty well. Perhaps I'd been wrong and it was Trudy after all. And where had her EpiPen gone?

"You there?" Levi asked, cutting into my thoughts.

"Yeah, yeah, I'm here. Say, listen, I'm gonna grab these cupcakes and get home. I'll see you tomorrow?"

"Call me when you get home. I want to be sure you made it okay and didn't fall asleep at the wheel. You've had a pretty traumatic day. I don't want you crashed into some snowbank somewhere."

"Okay, will do. Talk to you in about a half-hour."

As soon as I hung up, I saw Stan watching me expectantly. Was there no privacy, for Pete's sake?

"Everything okay there, Miss Melanie?" he asked. He rocked back on his heels, then his toes, his hands tucked in his front pockets.

"I sure hope so, Stan. I sure hope so."

"Been seeing more of you these past few days than I've seen you in a while."

I couldn't remember seeing him at all before Stormi asked him if he knew who played Santa for the Christmas festival. Maybe I merely hadn't paid attention since the bakery was the only thing in my line of sight.

"I'm only here to pick up some cupcakes Stormi left for me. She said she told you that I'd be by and that it was okay for me to go pick them up."

"Yup, she sure did. Thought it'd be earlier, though." He started walking toward the bakery in the back corner and waved at me to follow him. "Come on. I'll take you back there."

"You know, I'm fine if you have something else you need to do," I said, walking fast to catch up with him. "I know where they are."

"I never pass up a chance to walk with a pretty gal," he said, winking at me.

Yuk! It was dark in the bakery. The only light came from the rest of the store. "Honestly, Stan, I'm fine. I just want to grab them and leave."

"I really shouldn't let someone back there alone. I could lose my job over that." He stopped, sighed, and tugged at his sleeve. "I won't bother you with another word. I'll just keep 'er zipped." He twisted his fingers in front of his lips and mimed throwing away a key.

Great! I'd hurt his feelings. I sighed and was about to say something, and then remembered there was a killer still running around out there. That is if Trudy wasn't the killer as I'd initially expected. Heck, as Walker still suspects, by the sounds of it.

"No hard feelings, Stan. I'm just in a hurry is all. It's been a tough day, and I'm beat."

"Well, listen," he said, "you go on back and get what you need. I need to call home quick, say goodnight to my kids. But I'll be standing right over there." He pointed to the hallway leading to the employees only section. "Yell if you need anything." He turned on his heel and left.

I waved over my shoulder and shook my head. Stan's hurt feelings were not my concern right now. And at this point, I wished I'd just forgotten about the darn cupcakes and went home. They might be as cute as the dickens, but they turned into a bigger hassle than they were worth.

I slipped behind the bakery counter, snaked between the shelving in the large working area toward the walk-in cooler, my heels click-click-clicking on the shining floor tiles. Stormi kept her kitchen immaculate. I peeked over my shoulder to be sure Stan hadn't followed me. He was giving me the creeps tonight.

Relieved he was nowhere in sight, I pulled open the heavy steel door to the walk-in cooler, using both hands. The cupcakes were on the back shelf. I stacked the three plastic cartons on top of one another, four cupcakes in each, and turned to leave, kicking the heavy door closed with my heel. When I didn't hear it latch, I set the cartons down on the counter so I could put my weight into it, closing it securely. The last thing Stormi needed was a cooler full of spoiled food because I left the door ajar.

After it clicked, I pulled on the handle for extra measure before scooping up the cartons again. When the top one threatened to slide off, I grabbed for it. In the process, the back of my hand knocked over a glass bottle on the small counter next to the cooler. I scrambled to upright the bottle before the contents spilled, praying it didn't crack. When I did, the top carton slid off and into the giant garbage can. Ugh! "Melanie, you big clutz," I muttered. So much for those. Except leaving them in the trash wasn't an option. How would I ever explain that to Stormi? How insulting it would be to think I tossed them. Thankfully, Stormi's kitchen was squeaky clean, unlike Nick's bathroom had been, and the trash can was nearly empty.

I set the other cartons down to retrieve the one from the trash can and noticed my thumb and forefinger on the hand I used to set the bottle upright felt slick. I examined them. Oil? I lifted a finger to my nose and sniffed. It had the faintest aroma of—what was that? I picked up the bottle and turned it to see the label. Peanut oil! Levi's words replayed in my head: *The autopsy showed she had peanut oil in her digestive system.* But it wouldn't be at all unusual to find peanut oil in a bakery. *Would it?*

I picked up the bottle, unscrewed the cover, and peeked inside to see half the bottle gone. Was I overreacting? It was a small bottle after all. One recipe could easily have called for the amount that was missing. And yet something felt very wrong.

I set the bottle back down, noticing a set of keys and a pair of black fingerless gloves tucked in the corner. If the night guy had come in early, where was he? And where was Stan? The hair on the back of my neck stood at attention, and I scanned the area, feeling like someone was watching. I couldn't see or hear anyone. Only eerie silence. I picked up the keys looking for some sort of identification. Just three standard keys and a tiny plastic pistol. The fingerless gloves could have been for a man or a woman.

I mentally ran through the few employees that worked here. Joe, Suze, and Tim. All part-time. I tried to remember if I'd seen any of them out and about at the Christmas festival. Tim! He had been standing in line next to Patti. Hadn't he been the one to pick up Patti's diet soda bottle and hand it to her?

Gooseflesh prickled my arms, and it seemed my heart was pounding in my ears. If I remember right, Tim came in between midnight and one to get things ready for Stormi when she arrived at five. Did Tim poison Patti? But why?

I glanced around me again to be sure no one else was there. Particularly Stan or Tim. As weird as Stan was acting tonight, I hadn't ruled him out. He had full access to these things for several hours throughout the night when no one was here to see him.

I needed to call Levi and fill him in. As I fished the cupcake box from the bottom of the trash before I left, a crumpled piece of paper caught my attention. Not only was it a certificate, it was a duplicate of the baking contest certificate that listed Patti as the winner. This one had Stormi's name listed as—*runner up*? That didn't make any sense! There was no possible way Patti could win against Stormi in a baking contest.

So they were in the same contest. That didn't mean anything, right? Except Patti wasn't what I thought. And how wrongly I'd judged her. *Never judge a book by its cover, Melanie*, Nana had always told me.

I opened my purse and snagged my phone. I was just about to punch the number programmed for Levi and stopped when I heard someone behind me.

"Hey, Melanie. What are you doing here so late?"

I turned. "Stormi? I could ask you the same thing. You're always in bed by now, aren't you?" I kept my phone in my hand.

She pointed toward the keys and gloves. "Forgot those." She motioned toward the counter. "For the life of me, I couldn't recall where I'd put them and then got distracted. When I was going to bed is when I remembered. Thank goodness I keep a spare set in my purse. One of the keys is for the register. Even though I empty it every day and dump the money in the safe, I didn't want to leave it here," she rambled, snatching the keys and gloves from the counter.

"They were with a bottle of peanut oil." I held it up and forced a smile.

She shrugged a shoulder. "Tim probably left it out. I called Stan to let him know I'd be back. He didn't tell you?"

I shook my head. "No. Stormi, about Stan…"

"What about him?" she said, glancing at my hand. She stiffened and grabbed for the certificate, crumpling it up again before tucking it in her coat pocket. "What are you doing going through my trash?"

"You were in the same contest as Patti?" I asked.

She scowled. "How did you know Patti was in it?"

"I found a certificate matching this one at my salon with Patti listed as the first-place winner."

"Yeah, go figure," she said bitterly. That chick doesn't bake. She had someone bake them for her and claimed she did it."

"Why would she do that?" I asked.

"Why *wouldn't* she?" Stormi countered. "She has been tormenting me since eighth grade. You'd think she would have grown out of that, but nope." She let out a quiet, bitter laugh. "Any guy I ever dated she took from me. Any class I did well in, she'd cheat her way into doing better. Anything I ever did, she worked at taking from me." She flung her hand toward the cupcakes, still sitting on the counter. "I worked my butt off for years at being a baker, and along she comes and one-ups me *again*."

I nodded toward the peanut oil. "Did you know Patti was allergic to peanuts, Stormi?"

"Who didn't? We all used to joke about putting it in her milk at lunch in school. Heck, the girls she went to summer camp with even put it in her shampoo. Too bad someone told her before she used it."

My mouth hung open. "That is so mean!"

She shrugged and tossed her spare set of keys in her purse, overshooting. I reached to catch them, knocking her bag onto the floor. The contents spilled onto the shining white tile and scattered every which way. A thin tube resembling a magic marker, yellow label with black writing, rolled across the floor. I snatched it up right before it disappeared under one of the metal carts. I froze.

"Patti's EpiPen?" I gasped, my eyes darting from the pen to Stormi.

"I'm crushed. Why would you assume it's hers?" she asked.

"Who else would it belong to?"

She shrugged. "Me?"

"Are you denying it's Patti's?"

"No. I'm neither confirming nor denying."

"Stormi," I said, frowning and shaking my head, clearing the revelation beginning to form. The one I didn't want to see. "Did you kill Patti?"

She shook her head slowly, stared blankly into nothingness for a moment, and scoffed, "Melanie, you have no idea how mean she was. How sick and tired I was from the bullying." It appeared as though she might cry at any minute. But then the sadness cleared, replaced with self-righteous indignation. "When she took this contest from me, that was the last straw. I was so done! People like that—well, they don't deserve to be here."

"Stormi, you need to turn yourself in. You can't let someone else take the blame for what you did. You're better than that."

"I'm not losing everything I've accomplished because of that monster." Her eyes narrowed.

Her pain tugged at my heart as I tried to make myself comprehend that she was a murderer.

"If you turn yourself in, I won't have to. Please," I begged.

She reached behind her back, pulled a gun from her waistband, and pointed it at me. I stared in disbelief. *Again? Does everyone carry a gun these days or what?* I thought, desperately trying to come up with a way out of this.

"Stormi," I said, as calm as I could, hands up, palms facing her, "you don't want to do this."

"Do what? I'm not going to kill you, Melanie. You're my friend. I've always liked you." She wiped a tear from her cheek with the back of her hand. "You've always been so nice to me."

"You're hurting, I get that," I said, trying to buy time. "You have a reason to. But, Stormi—"

"Hand me your phone." She held her hand out to me, palm facing up, and wiggled her fingers. "And then you're going to go into the cooler while I get the heck out of here and disappear."

"Tim comes in at midnight?" I asked.

"He called in sick. His kids got the flu."

I was at the doorway to the cooler and beginning to panic. "I'll freeze to death in there."

"Open it," she ordered, brushing a tear from her cheek with the back of her hand.

"Stormi—" I pleaded.

"I said open it. If you had just minded your own business, Melanie, no one would be the wiser, and we could all go on with life as usual. I have to admit, I'm a little peeved that you ruined things for me. All because of a bully. *I'm* the victim here!" She poked her thumb at her chest. "Me! I thought you were my friend. Friends don't turn on friends."

She jerked the gun to get me to speed things up a bit. I yanked on the door when I felt the tip of the gun on my back. With strength I didn't know I had, I pulled it back hard while twisting enough to knock her arm with my elbow. The gun clattered across the floor, skittering under the metal cabinet.

She yelped, grasped her face with her hand, and dropped my phone. As I reached for it and stood back up, Stan appeared in front of me.

"What in the heck is going on back here?" he said. "Stormi, you okay?" He raced toward her and pulled out a handkerchief, holding it up to her bleeding nose.

"She went crazy, Stan!" Stormi said, holding the now red hanky tightly to her face. "Arrest her!"

Stan appeared dumbfounded. "I'm not a cop, Stormi. I can't arrest people."

"What good are you, then?" she shouted, making Stan bristle.

"Hey, that's not fair! I called you like you asked me to if she got here before you. I tried to stall her but — but — well, I stalled her as long as I could," he said, his eyes begging for her forgiveness.

But there was no time for Stormi to forgive him. Through my emotional whiplash from starting my day early, being held at gunpoint not once, but twice, that day, the injustice of Stan being Stormi's accomplice, learning my friend was a killer, and sheer fatigue, I became vaguely aware of a sea of black and blue as officers appeared from the front and the back door. Apparently, someone called 911. Good thing, because when Stormi dropped my phone, it broke.

Again. Me and cell phones were having a hard time getting along this week. At this rate, I could own stock in the phone company.

"Stormi, why did you need Stan to let you know if I got here first?"

"I knew the bottle of oil was by my gloves and keys," she said. She set her gun down on the counter. "Guess I lost."

Walker turned the corner and locked eyes with me.

He shook his head in resignation. "Figured you were involved," he grumbled. "Levi's on his way."

29

Claire and I helped Nana with the final touches on Christmas Eve dinner while Sydney chased poor Callie Cat around the house. Just as she found the big furball, Callie managed to slip away and hide again. I'm not sure how the fat cat did so, but apparently she wanted to escape badly enough to make it happen.

In an effort to keep Rubie out of the kitchen, I tasked her with keeping Levi entertained. And she was doing an excellent job of it by telling him stories from her Norwegian family. I caught snippets over the kitchen noise, Syd's frustration with Callie Cat, and Levi's occasional laughter. For the most part, whenever I peeked in the living room, I caught him staring at her with amused disbelief. Cole and Scott both had the Christmas Eve shift at work, but both also had Christmas Day off to spend with family.

Christmas Eve had always been my favorite celebration because it brought back so many good memories of Granddad. Nana always made dinner, and we ate until we thought we'd all pop. Then we sat around the tree, only the Christmas lights glowing in the room as she read the story of Christ's birth from the book of Luke. I remembered feeling so safe and loved. After she finished reading, we opened presents. But the opening presents part wasn't the most important to me, even as a kid. It was all of us together in the lights, the music, the Christmas love.

"Is it almost time to eat?" Sydney said as she slid on stocking feet through the kitchen entryway.

"Sydney Rae," Claire scolded, "do be careful. You almost ran smack into Grandma Rose."

My grandmother smiled, her periwinkle eyes twinkling as she wrapped an arm around Sydney's shoulders. "Almost, dear. Why don't you let old Callie sleep for a while and start putting things on the table?"

"Sounds like a plan, Grandma," Sydney said with her cute lisp. It was getting less noticeable as she got older, but I hoped it never went entirely away. It was sweet as could be.

When everything was ready, Claire, Nana, and I all stood back to admire the table. It was picture perfect. Sydney wedged her way in between Claire and Nana with an arm around each.

"Let's eat!" she announced.

All settled into our places, Nana said grace before the reaching, scooping, laughing, plopping, and drinking began. I took a moment to sit quietly and take in the beauty of the table—Nana's Christmas napkins folded just so, her Christmas table cloth adorned with bowls and plates of homemade cranberry sauce, cornbread muffins, green bean casserole, a gorgeous honeyed ham, and a turkey that appeared to be plucked straight from a magazine. I watched as Levi stood to carve the meat, his black tactical pants—always the cop—and black and red button-up shirt, sleeves rolled up. I gazed at each of these special people in my life while appreciating being right here, right now, at this very moment.

"Are you okay, dear?" Nana asked as she leaned over toward me.

"What's wrong, Aunt Mel?" Sydney asked, her eyes enormous pools of concern.

I hadn't realized until then that there were tears in my eyes.

"Nothing's wrong," I said, smiling as I pulled my sleeves over my hands and dabbed my eyes. "I'm just so happy."

I beheld Levi, earning a wink that made me weak in the knees. And then Rubie, bless her heart, brought the fun back to the moment.

"Hey, Levi," she said, "how come you don't have to work tonight, but you're making my man work? And Cole."

"I didn't make them work," he said. "It's a matter of being on patrol versus in the Detective Division."

"Cole has tomorrow off," Claire said. "We're going to have a quiet Christmas Day at my house so Syd can have some time to play with her things."

"What things?" I grinned. "From Santa?"

Rubie groaned. "Oh, man! Don't mention Santa." She popped her hand over her mouth and stared at Sydney. "Sorry!"

"It's okay," Sydney said, sounding eighteen instead of nine. "I don't believe in Santa anymore."

"If there's a homicide tonight, Levi will get called out and have to leave. So everyone in Birch Haven better be on their best behavior," I said.

"No worries there," Claire said, grinning. "You're here, so the town is safe, and Birch Haven PD should have a silent night."

"Rude!" I said, making a face at her.

"Hey," Rubie said to me as she piled mashed potatoes on her plate, "you never finished filling me in on how Stormi got the peanut oil to Patti."

I looked at Levi. "Wanna take this one?"

He shook his head and said, "Nope," before biting into a mouthful of cornbread. "I'm off duty."

I took a deep breath. "Well," I said, "turns out Patti went to the bakery before coming over to the salon. To rub Stormi's face in the fact that she'd lost the baking contest. She even admitted to Stormi that she'd hired someone else to bake the cupcakes for her."

"What happened to them, by the way?" Rubie asked before spooning gravy onto her potatoes.

"Far as I know, they're still there," I said.

"She probably poisoned them," Rubie said.

I shook my head slowly, thinking of Stormi. I couldn't help but feel sad for her. "No, she wouldn't have done that. She was a victim of bullying and finally broke after so many years."

"Babe," Levi said, turning my chin to look at him, "do not feel sorry for her. She almost killed you."

"Didn't they have to bake the cupcakes there? At the place?" Rubie said, scrunching up her nose. "That seems a little sketchy."

"Apparently not. Anyhow," I continued, "Stormi was over it. The bullying. She told Patti she just wanted to let it go, let bygones be bygones, and offered her a bottle of soda from the soda cooler beside the front bakery counter as a truce. After Stormi got it from the cooler, she made some excuse to leave for a second and slipped the peanut oil in the soda. She returned to where Patti was waiting for her, opened the bottle so Patti wouldn't know she had already opened it, and handed it to her." I glanced at Levi. "Premeditated, huh, babe?"

He smirked. "I could never have told it like you, Blondie."

"Wouldn't she have seen the oil in the soda?" Rubie asked.

"Maybe the wrapper on the bottle didn't allow it. And I don't know about you, but when I take a drink from a bottle I don't study it first."

"So, are you expecting Santa to visit you this year?" Rubie said. "I'm not so sure you've been a good girl."

I shook my head. "I invited him, but he said he wouldn't be caught dead at my house."

"Oh, Mel, that was terrible!" Nana exclaimed, but chuckled.

"That was so bad!"

"Booo!"

They all said at the same time, laughing hysterically. Eventually, we all settled down to a content state. I raised my glass, and the rest followed.

"Merry Christmas," I said, looking from one to the next to the next. I leaned my head against my grandmother's and whispered, "And a very special Merry Christmas to you, Nana. You're my Christmas angel."

Sugar Cookies

<u>Ingredients:</u>
1 ½ cups powdered sugar
1 cup butter
1 egg
2 ½ cups sifted flour
1 tsp cream of tartar
1 tsp baking soda
1 tsp vanilla
½ tsp almond extract

Beat butter and sugar together; add egg and flavorings; add dry ingredients. Refrigerate 2-3 hours. Roll out dough on floured surface and cut out cookies with cookie cutters. Bake on greased cookie sheet for 7-8 minutes in a 375-degree oven. (It isn't necessary to re-grease sheets between batches because the cookies contain enough butter to keep the pans greased.)

Note: If the dough is too sticky while rolling out, add more flour or return to refrigerator for a time.

Frosting Ingredients:
2 lbs. powdered sugar

2/3 cup milk

1 tsp vanilla

Pinch of salt

Food coloring, optional

One batch makes 50 cookies. I don't usually measure the frosting ingredients, just fill several bowls with powdered sugar, add milk with a dab of vanilla until the frosting is the right consistency. Then add food coloring to each bowl to make different colors of frosting. Then I ask the children to decorate!

❖ *Karen Whalen*

Southern Cheese Straws

<u>Ingredients:</u>
1 block extra sharp cheese
2 sticks margarine (Parkay brand)
1 tbsp sugar
1 tsp salt
½ tsp paprika
½ tsp red pepper
4-5 drops tabasco

Grate cheese. Beat cheese with margarine until creamy. Sift together dry ingredients. Slowly add to cheese mixture. Put in old fashioned cookie press. Press out small medallions. Bake at 350 degrees for 25 minutes on parchment paper.

❖ *Jenn Jones*

German Lebkuchen Cookies

Ingredients:
1 egg
¾ cup brown sugar
½ cup honey
½ cup dark molasses
3 cups sifted all-purpose flour
½ tsp baking soda
1¼ tsp ground nutmeg
1¼ tsp ground cinnamon
½ tsp ground cloves
½ tsp ground allspice
½ cup slivered almonds
½ cup candied mixed fruit peel, finely chopped
1 egg white beaten
1 tbsp lemon juice
½ tsp lemon zest
1½ cups sifted confectioner's sugar

Preheat oven to 350 degrees and grease two baking sheets or line with parchment paper.

Sift together the flour, nutmeg, cinnamon, cloves, and allspice. Set aside.

Beat the egg and sugar together on medium speed until light and fluffy, about two minutes. Scrape down the bowl.

Beat in the honey and molasses until thoroughly combined.

On low speed, stir in the flour mixture until just combined.

Place the dough on a well-floured surface and knead, adding more flour as you knead.

Wrap the dough in plastic wrap and chill until firm, about two hours or overnight.

On a well-floured surface, roll out the dough into a 9x12-inch rectangle. Cut the dough into 18 3x2-inch rectangles.

Bake for 10-12 minutes.

Transfer the cookies to a wire rack and let cool. Whisk together the confectioner's sugar, water, and lemon juice, and brush or spread on top of the cookies.

Allow glaze to firm and then store the cookies in an airtight container at room temperature.

❖ *Steve Linde*

Overnight Baked Croissant French Toast Casserole

Ingredients:
8 large croissants, cubed
6 large eggs, beaten
¾ cup heavy cream
¼ cup egg nog
2 tsp vanilla
1 tsp ground cinnamon
½ tsp nutmeg
¼ cup sugar
¾ cup brown sugar
½ tsp salt

Preheat oven to 350 degrees.
Prepare a 9x13 pan with cooking spray.
In a large bowl mix eggs, heavy cream, egg nog, sugars, vanilla, salt, cinnamon, nutmeg. Beat slightly.
Cube croissants and place in prepared 9x13 pan.
Pour over egg mixture (or you can dip each cubed piece in egg mixture and place in pan, then pour the remaining egg mixture over). Allow to soak.
At this point, you can cover with plastic wrap and place in refrigerate overnight to bake in the morning or place in oven right away to bake 45 min-1 hour

(time depends on density of bread used). Add any extras (below) or toppings if you wish prior to baking. Serve warm with syrup.

Optional variations:
Pair:
Zest of an orange & 1½ tsp Grand Marnier

In place of croissant:
Apple fritters or French bread or cinnamon bread

Optional add-ins:
Apple pie filling or blueberries, raspberries, strawberries or sliced bananas w/ chopped walnuts & pecans.

❖ *Kerri Keprios*

Dear Reader,

Word of mouth is the best promotion for an author. Please consider leaving a review on Amazon and Goodreads. A sentence or two is all that is needed. By doing this, it helps me, as the author, as well as other readers.

I would love for you to connect with me at:

Website: rhondablackhurst.com
Email: rjblackhurst0611@gmail.com
Facebook: www.facebook.com/rjblackhurst
Twitter: @rjblackhurst
Instagram: Rhonda.blackhurst

Best,
    Rhonda

Acknowledgements

The industry of independent publishing has been filled with twists and turns through the years, as well as tremendous growth in popularity. It has achieved the respect that the early pioneers didn't get. While many refer to it as self-publishing, that is an inaccurate term because it is far from a solo process. It is comprised of a lot of hard work and a team of people, the author being only one person on that team.

I extend my deepest gratitude to the following people in my tribe:

Rachel Olson (No Sweat Graphics & Formatting)—for your creativity in designing my covers and formatting my words. Thank you for taking my vision and making it beautiful.

Jessica Cornwell (Jessica Cornwell Author Services)—for your expertise in taking my story and making it shine.

Sandy Hilger—Your skill as a beta reader goes above and beyond and far exceeds any expectations I could have.

Sisters in Crime and Sisters in Crime Colorado Chapter, Northern Colorado Writers, and Rocky

Mountain Fiction Writers—for community, inspiration, and motivation.

My Camp NaNo cabinmates, Kit Dunsmore and Liam Rooney—for sharing the joy and heartache of the writing process, and for the motivation to keep on keepin' on.

Karen Whalen—for our weekly writing get-togethers and so much more. I appreciate you more than you know.

My dad and mom—a special thanks to you for teaching me the true "reason for the season." For making Christmas such a special time of my childhood and beginning the tradition of reading the story of Christ's birth from the book of Luke every year before we could open presents.

Clint, Ben, Alex, and Jennifer—for being my whole world. You're my sun on cloudy days, and my rainbow in the rain. Thank you for far more than I could ever say.

About the Author

Rhonda was born in northern Minnesota but now resides in Colorado with her husband, and close to her children and grandchildren. Though she fully enjoys the Rocky Mountains, a piece of her heart will always belong to the woods and lakes of Minnesota.

Her love of writing took flight at the tender age of four when she was caught writing with her crayons on the knotty pine walls of the family home. In her teens, she tested her hand at journalism by writing an article or two for the city newspaper about school events. She completed a Journalism/Short Story Writing course and was a stringer for a local newspaper, writing about school and community events.

When she's not at her day job as a Restitution Advocate in a District Attorney's Office, she can be found hibernating in her home office creating characters, settings, and stories. When she's not writing, she's reading books on the craft of writing, and is typically reading more than one fiction book at a time. Mostly mysteries, of course.

www.ingramcontent.com/pod-product-compliance
Lightning Source LLC
Chambersburg PA
CBHW072115250626
47159CB00007B/2462